James was too late! The thieves leaped aboard the
helicopter, taking Tracy and the jeweled sword with
them. Even before the door was shut, the machine
began to lift off of the roof.

The wind from the swirling blades whipped at
James's eyes as he desperately jumped for the helicopter. He couldn't let them get away! His fingers
clawed for a grip and locked around the closer of the
copter's skis. Grimly he hung on as the copter continued to rise.

Sword of Death

John Vincent

PUFFIN BOOKS

PUFFIN BOOKS

Published by the Penguin Group

Penguin Books USA Inc., 375 Hudson Street, New York, New York 10014, U.S.A.

Penguin Books Ltd, 27 Wrights Lane, London W8 5TZ, England

Penguin Books Australia Ltd, Ringwood, Victoria, Australia

Penguin Books Canada Ltd, 10 Alcorn Avenue, Toronto, Ontario, Canada M4V 3B2

Penguin Books (N.Z.) Ltd, 182–190 Wairau Road, Auckland 10, New Zealand

Penguin Books Ltd, Registered Offices: Harmondsworth, Middlesex, England

First published in the United States of America by Puffin Books,
a division of Penguin Books USA Inc., 1992

1   3   5   7   9   10   8   6   4   2

Printed in the United States of America
Set in Cheltenham Book

Sword of Death

Chapter One
Ninja Attack

The Warfield Academy van came to a stop just outside the British Museum. Tracy Milbanks jumped eagerly to her feet.

"Come on," she told her friends. "Let's go!"

James Bond Jr. glanced at the third member of their group, Horace ("IQ") Boothroyd. Even though James and IQ shared a dorm room, they were as different as night and day. James was dark-haired and athletic—and always ready for adventure. IQ was fair-haired and skinny—and always ready to stick his nose in a book. IQ was such a brain, in fact, that he usually even dressed like a scientist.

But today IQ had given up his lab coat, and instead wore a neat blue blazer with a single rose pinned to his lapel. This was completely out of the ordinary for

IQ, whose only interest in flowers was in biology class.

"It must be nice being the headmaster's daughter," James said to Tracy. "You can get class trips arranged just so you can see the new exhibits of Japanese art that you're so crazy about."

"It's very educational," Tracy said with a wink. "Will you two *please* hurry up? There'll be a huge line if we don't get there soon."

Tracy had always loved Japanese art and she had no intention of missing this display of rare artifacts. Even if she practically had to drag her friends along to see it. As they walked quickly through the rooms and corridors Tracy kept looking over her shoulder to make sure James and IQ were still with her. James waved to reassure her they were still there, then stuck out his tongue when she turned around. Tracy had not been able to convince their other two friends, Gordon ("Gordo") Leiter and Phoebe Farragut, to come with them. Gordo had no interest at all in museums, and Phoebe had explained that she didn't like looking at stuff she couldn't buy.

"How come you're so dressed up today?" James asked IQ. "Did Tracy threaten you or something?"

"I just needed a lapel for my rose," IQ replied. He frowned. "For some reason they don't make lab-coat lapels with buttonholes."

"Not much call for it, I guess," James said with a smile. Sometimes IQ was completely out of touch with the real world. As usual, he wasn't making much sense, either. "Anyway, most people wear carnations, you know," was all James said.

"This isn't a real rose," IQ began, but Tracy cut him off.

"Will you stop talking and hurry up?" she asked impatiently. "At the rate you're going, it'll be closed by the time we get there!"

"Relax, Tracy," James said. "We'll be there in a minute. Here it is now." Ahead hung a colorful banner announcing the Japanese exhibit.

As soon as they entered Tracy's eyes lit up. She rushed ahead to a large case in the center of the room. Inside a tall mannequin dressed in ceremonial *samurai* armor and helmet glared fiercely. A bright curved sword was clutched in its raised fist. The handle of the sword was covered with jewels, which sparkled brilliantly in the light.

"Oh, James," Tracy sighed happily. "Isn't that sword fabulous?"

James knew that it was more than just a beautiful sword. "Incredible," he agreed. "I believe it was used by Minamoto Yoritomo. He was the first *shogun*, a powerful warrior who ruled Japan around twelve hundred A. D., if I remember my history right."

"It was eleven ninety-two A. D., actually," IQ said. He could never resist correcting a little mistake. "It's an unusual weapon for that period."

"The jewels are intense, aren't they?" Tracy asked. "They must be worth a fortune."

"Jewels!" IQ said, slapping his forehead. "I knew

3

there was something I'd forgotten!" He reached into his blazer pocket and, to everyone's surprise, pulled out a pair of earrings. They appeared to be made of gold, with two small diamonds in each one. "Try these on, Tracy."

Tracy stared at them. "Why, IQ!" she exclaimed. "It's not my birthday or anything. What are these for?"

"Just put them on," IQ told her. "And I'll explain." He took a small box from his pocket. There was a digital readout on the top of it. "Those are experimental biosensors."

Tracy clipped the earrings onto her lobes. "So what?"

The display on the box lit up and showed a figure of seventy-two. "Your heart rate," IQ explained. "A bit high, because you're excited. But while you have them on, I'll be able to monitor your health."

"It's nice of you to be so concerned," Tracy said. "But I feel perfectly fine."

"If they work," IQ said, "then I can fit James with similar monitors. That way, we'll be able to keep track of him and tell if he's in trouble."

James chuckled. "Thanks, IQ, but they're not exactly my style."

IQ laughed. "I was thinking that maybe a ring would be more your taste."

Tracy walked off to look into another case. This one held small figures elaborately carved from ivory and jade.

"Ne-tsu-ke!" she said.

"Bless you," James teased.

"That's what these are called, James," Tracy told him, rolling her eyes. "They're from the Tokugawa period, I think, dated about—"

A shrill alarm suddenly interrupted her. Everyone in the room stopped studying the displays and looked around, wondering what had set off the bell. As James spun around he saw something flash past his face. Whatever it was hit the glass case surrounding the *shogun* model and shattered the glass into splinters. When it finally fell harmlessly to the floor amid the debris, James got a good look at it.

"What was that?" IQ yelped, shaking glass splinters off himself.

"A throwing star," James said grimly.

"But where'd it come from?" asked Tracy, staring at the wrecked case.

"Taking a wild guess," James said, "I'd say from them." He pointed upward.

The huge skylight in the ceiling of the gallery had been pried open. A thick rope dangled from the opening. As James and his friends looked on, an amazingly quick and silent team of masked men slid down the rope.

There were three of them. Each wore a black mask with slits for his eyes, and each carried an assortment of Ninja weapons. *Nunchakus,* deadly *sai* swords, and more throwing stars dangled from their belts. All were dressed completely in black.

Just as the last Ninja reached the end of the rope, the museum guards rushed in. "Hey!" one guard yelled.

The Ninja leader barely looked at the men, then flicked his wrist. A throwing star sliced through the room. The razor-sharp edges neatly severed the ropes of a Japanese fishing net that hung above the entryway. The net collapsed, trapping the guards beneath it.

People in the gallery had started to panic. Some scrambled for cover; others tried to run.

Without even thinking, James started for the Ninja warriors. The leader looked like he was doing something to the *shogun* mannequin that had been in the shattered case. His backups instantly dropped into fighting crouches. Their hands went to their belts.

James was ready for them. He grabbed one of the wooden information signs scattered throughout the gallery. He swung it up in front of himself like a shield just as something hit the wood with a couple of *thunks.* The tips of two knives, honed to a deadly sharpness, poked through, micrometers from James's chest.

James swung the sign around as hard as he could and rushed forward. It slammed into the two Ninjas, who went sprawling.

"Enjoy your trip," James told them politely before spinning to check on the Ninja leader.

Quick as lightning, the leader snatched the jeweled sword from the mannequin and stuck it through the sash around his waist. As James started to run toward him he whirled and jumped for the rope still hanging from the skylight. His two backups joined him in swiftly climbing toward the ceiling.

James reached the rope and began hoisting himself up after them. The Ninjas were impossibly fast, though. By the time James was five feet off the ground, they'd already reached the top.

The Ninja leader looked back and saw James. He drew the jeweled sword and slashed the rope. James fell to the floor, landing on his back.

"This way!" Tracy yelled from across the room. She'd opened an emergency exit door and found stairs leading to the roof. "We can still cut them off."

"They just cut *me* off," James muttered. He scrambled to his feet and started after Tracy. She burst through the door and raced up the steps with IQ right behind her. James sprinted past IQ and burst out onto the flat roof. Tracy was way ahead of him, chasing the three Ninjas.

"Tracy!" James yelled. "Watch out! Don't try to stop them!"

The three men were racing toward a black helicopter perched on the edge of the roof. Its rotor was spinning, ready to lift off the second they were aboard. James wasn't surprised to see that they had their escape planned.

At James's shout, the leader spun around. Seeing Tracy almost on them, he stopped abruptly. When Tracy finally caught up with him, his hand flashed out and grabbed her neck. Tracy's eyes fluttered closed, and she collapsed. The Ninja scooped her up in his arms and set off again for the copter.

Even though he was running at top speed, James knew he was too late. The three thieves leaped aboard the helicopter, taking Tracy and the sword with them. Even before the door was shut, the rotor sped up and the machine lifted off the roof.

The wind from the swirling blades whipped at James's eyes as he desperately jumped for the helicopter. He couldn't let them get away with kidnapping Tracy! His fingers clawed for a grip and locked around the closer of the copter's skis. Grimly he hung on as the copter continued to rise. Then he was swinging in the air.

The helicopter started to move away from the roof of the British Museum. James fought to swing his legs up for a better grip on the ski. The Ninja leader caught sight of him and with a furious growl pushed the door open again. Drawing the jeweled sword, he aimed a vicious blow straight at James's fingers.

Chapter Two
Midnight Madness

As the blade swooped toward him James realized he had no choice.

He let go.

If he'd held on, he reasoned, the sword would have sliced off his fingers, and he would have fallen anyway. The trouble was, now he was heading for a hard landing—fast! As he dropped like a brick he closed his eyes and prayed that something would break his fall. Maybe someone had left an old mattress lying around, or a spare trampoline . . .

Squish!

James had landed. The shock of landing confused his brain a little, because he thought at first the squishing noise was himself being smashed into a pulp. Then he realized he could still move his arms and legs. He was alive! He opened his eyes.

Yuck! He'd landed in the Dumpster that was parked behind the museum's restaurant. The leftover spaghetti, old potato peels, used tea bags, and other junk had made for a pretty soft landing. But phew! They smelled terrible, and now so did James.

James stood up, picking brown lettuce leaves and bread crusts off his T-shirt and jeans. "I guess lunch is on me," he muttered to himself. He stared upward and squinted. He could barely see the helicopter as it vanished. It was heading north, he noticed. Tracy was now a prisoner. But what would those Ninjas do with her? Let her go, or kill her?

James sighed as he climbed out of the trash. He knew that Tracy had handled dangerous situations before, but he had an awful feeling that this time they had stumbled onto something really evil.

The Warfield Academy van was parked outside the gate. James headed toward it with a heavy step—and a heavier heart.

"Why, hello, Bond," an unmistakable voice greeted him. "I see you've finally found your place in life: with the rubbish!"

James looked up to see the most obnoxious person he'd ever met—and the last person he wanted to see—standing before him. James didn't know what Trevor Noseworthy was doing in London, and he didn't care.

Both Trevor and James attended the exclusive, tightly guarded boarding school. The kids who went there were all pretty different from one another, but

11

all had one thing in common: parents who were very rich, or very important, or very both.

James was there because of who his uncle was. His namesake Uncle James was the most celebrated spy the world had ever known. At the very least, young James was considered a terrorist target. In any case, his reasons for being at Warfield had certainly been proved valid by his experiences since getting there.

Trevor had had it in for James ever since James had started at Warfield. He just couldn't get used to the idea that James was more athletic, smarter, more popular, more *everything* than Trevor. The fact that Trevor had never been close to being any of those things didn't matter. Trevor spent most of his time trying to figure out rotten tricks to play on James. The fact that they usually backfired onto Trevor only made him hate James more.

"I say, James," Trevor went on, "cat got your tongue? My, my, what atrocious aftershave you're wearing. It's a wonder you haven't been arrested for air pollution." He laughed like a crazy hyena at his own idiotic joke.

James was in such a fog of misery he didn't care. He just pushed Trevor aside. In doing so, he accidentally left a smelly smear of pea soup on Trevor's prissy sport coat.

"My jacket!" Trevor fumed. "You'll pay for this, Bond! I mean it this time!" He hurried off, frantically brushing at his sleeve and muttering something about finding a dry cleaner.

IQ came running up to James. He was completely

winded and couldn't talk. "James," he gasped, after a minute. "You're all right! But where's Tracy?"

"Those Ninjas have her, I'm afraid," James replied grimly. "But we'll get her back safely, I promise. I just wish I knew how." Then he remembered the earrings IQ had given her. "IQ—your biosensors! We can use them like homing devices and follow her."

"I wish we could, but they're not made for that," IQ said. "They'll show us whether or not she's alive, though, as long as she's still within range." He took the monitor from his pocket. The digital display now read eighty-four. "She's not far off. Her heart's beating awfully fast," IQ said, "but at least it's beating."

"She must be scared stiff," James said softly.

"I wrote down the registration number of the helicopter," IQ told him. "It must be on record. If we can find out who owns it—"

"Then we'll have a lead on Tracy." James patted his friend on the back. "Good work, IQ. How long will it take you?"

"I have to get to my computer back at school," IQ said. "Then I can get into the flight computer at Heathrow and track the copter. Twenty minutes, tops."

"It's going to be a long trip back to school," James sighed.

"Maybe we should call the police and pass on what we know," IQ suggested.

"If they see the cops, the Ninjas might just decide to kill Tracy and make a quick getaway," James pointed out. "I think she'll have a better chance if we try to get her back ourselves."

Nodding, IQ climbed into the van. "And with Gordo and Phoebe back at Warfield," he said, "we do have some reinforcements we can call in."

James squelched after IQ and sat down next to him.

As soon as they were back at Warfield, James took a long, hot shower. By the time he was finished, IQ had tapped into the flight computer. The young genius looked up from his terminal with a sparkle of excitement in his eyes.

"According to the official records," he told James, "that helicopter is owned by a firm called Gnome Electronics. It was supposed to be making a trip to the Chelsea Heliport, but called in with motor trouble."

"Well, now they've got Bond trouble," James answered. "Where is this Gnome Electronics located?"

"Just down the coast from here," IQ told him. "About five miles."

"Good." James nodded. "I don't suppose that Gnome happened to report the helicopter stolen or anything?"

"No." IQ smiled. "In fact, I did a little checking into Gnome Electronics while I was at it. It seems that they are a small importing firm. They were bought out only two months ago by a Japanese group, the Kawa Company."

"That's interesting," James said. "A Japanese company . . . I'm sure you know that Ninjas were highly disciplined assassins back in Japan's feudal era. And those men at the museum stole an ancient Japanese

14

sword." He shook his head. "I'm afraid it's not getting any clearer, but it does seem as if everything is linked together." He made up his mind. "IQ—you go and get Gordo. I'll see if I can get Mr. Mitchell's permission to take an evening drive . . ."

Buddy Mitchell was Warfield's gym instructor. He had been an undercover agent until a few years ago when his cover had been blown. Or so he said. Mr. Mitchell claimed he was retired from active duty, but James didn't totally believe him. Although he liked the tall, muscular teacher, James still wasn't sure just how much he trusted him. In the past James had found that whenever he happened to mention something he needed to Mr. Mitchell, whatever it was "coincidentally" turned up. It was helpful; still, James thought the gym teacher might have his own motives for the things he did. Motives that had nothing to do with helping James. Or not especially so, anyway.

When he found Mr. Mitchell, James asked about getting a special pass to leave campus. Because of the nature of its student body, Warfield had a sophisticated security system to keep out intruders. At the same time it also kept the students *in*. Sometimes James, who often needed to be off campus, could get away by simply requesting a pass. At other times he had to resort to sneaking out past the security system. He preferred to do it the easy way whenever possible. And at Warfield it was actually easier to sneak out than to ask permission from their rigid headmaster, Mr. Milbanks. Sometimes it was hard to believe that grouchy, nitpicking Mr. Milbanks was really the father of friendly, easygoing Tracy. But he was.

When he heard James's request, Mr. Mitchell frowned. "You just got back to school, James," he pointed out. "Mr. Milbanks is in a pretty difficult mood right now."

If only Mr. Milbanks wasn't such a stickler for the rules, not to mention Tracy's father. Tracy! James shuddered to think what Mr. Milbanks would say if he knew where his daughter was now. IQ had been all for telling him, but James had persuaded him to keep quiet about it. If Mr. Milbanks knew his daughter was missing, he'd probably have the police, the army, and anyone else he could think of looking for Tracy. And that could be very hazardous to her health.

James was as worried as he could be about getting Tracy back safe and sound. But he wanted to try to rescue her his way before giving in and pressing the panic button.

"I'd rather the headmaster didn't know about this trip," was all James told Mr. Mitchell.

The gym teacher raised an eyebrow.

James gave him what he hoped was an innocent look.

Mr. Mitchell sighed and handed James a pass. "All right, but keep this between us, James. For *both* our sakes."

It was dark outside by the time James reached the parking lot. IQ and Gordo were loading things into the trunk of James's red sports car. They both looked up as James came over.

"Hey, my man," Gordo said with a grin. As usual, he was dressed in jams and a wild Hawaiian shirt. His long blond hair hung down to his shoulders and his sneakers were untied. "All set to rock and roll?"

Gordo's dad, Felix Leiter, was a secret agent who often worked with James's uncle. Gordo had been raised in California and loved the sun, the sand, and most of all, surfing—none of which he could find at Warfield. He had to get most of his fun helping James on his adventures.

"As soon as you two are finished," James said, "we can be on our way." He looked at the two cases still not stowed in the trunk. "We're not going far, IQ. Don't you think you may have overpacked a little?"

IQ pointed at the bags. "This isn't clothes, James. I just packed one or two items that might be useful if we decide to break into Gnome's offices."

"One or two items?" James echoed. "IQ, with all the stuff you've brought, we could probably break into the Tower of London and steal the crown jewels." Then he sighed. "Well, let's get going. I've got a feeling this is going to be a very long night . . ."

Chapter Three
There's No Place Like Gnome

It was past midnight by the time James rolled to a stop and parked. Gnome Electronics was in an industrial park on the outskirts of the coastal city of Dover. The main building had three floors, and was made of glass and metal. James parked behind a small building next door. There were likely to be security guards around, and he didn't want his convertible to be seen.

"What do you think, IQ?" he asked. "It looks pretty quiet."

IQ shrugged. "I'd be surprised if they didn't have state-of-the-art security devices," he replied. "Fortunately, the more sophisticated things are, the easier it is for me to get past them." He took two pairs of sunglasses out of one of the suitcases. He handed one to James, and put the other pair over his own glasses.

"Wrong time of the day to catch some rays," Gordo said helpfully.

"These aren't normal sunglasses, Gordo," IQ replied.

James grinned. "I'd have been disappointed if they were. So what do they do?"

"Well, most security systems use either infrared detectors or ultraviolet beams. Both are invisible to the eye, so we would walk right into such systems and set off the alarms." He pointed to a switch set in the side of the glasses. "This control alters the sensitivity of the sunglasses. It will allow us to see normally, infrared, and ultraviolet. You control the settings like this." IQ demonstrated. "This way we can avoid triggering the alarms."

James put his pair on. He could see perfectly through them. Then he tried the infrared setting, which showed heat instead of light. The ground was a fuzzy red color, and both IQ and Gordo were bright orange, like walking lightbulbs. He studied the office building, scanning windows and doorways. No alarms were visible in infrared. He set the glasses to ultraviolet.

James could instantly see long bars of light crisscrossing the lawn. This place was well prepared for unwanted visitors!

"Looks like it's Gnome-man's land," he muttered.

IQ grinned. "Since we can see the alarm beams, all

we have to do is step over them." He looked apologetically at Gordo. "But I only have two pairs."

"You'd better stay with the car," James told Gordo. "We may need to get out of here double time, so be ready." He pointed to a small light on the dashboard. "IQ's linked this circuit by radio to my watch. If we're in trouble, I'll signal you. The light will flash, and you'd better come running."

"No problemo, my man," Gordo agreed. He settled into the driver's seat. "Meantime, I'll catch a few z's. We athletic types need our beauty sleep."

"Just as long as you come if we need you," James told him.

"Trust me," Gordo replied, eyes closed and feet on the dashboard. "I'm ready to leap into action at a second's notice."

James shook his head and then turned back to IQ. "Grab whatever you think we'll need and let's go."

IQ opened his cases and rummaged through them. He handed James a small device that looked like a TV remote control. James slipped it into his pocket. Then IQ passed him a small gunlike device that had what seemed to be a fishing reel attached to it. Finally, he put a couple of other things into his labcoat pockets. To James's astonishment, IQ then pulled out his rose and stuck it into his pocket, too.

"You don't need a flower to break into a factory," James said.

IQ smiled. "This isn't an ordinary flower," he replied. "It's—" He broke off as a low snore came from Gordo. "Some lookout," he muttered.

"Let's just hope we don't need him," James answered. "Come on." He led the way across the lawn.

The alarm beams were perfectly clear through the special lenses. James carefully stepped over the glowing bars and made his way to the front door of the large building. The sign above the glass entrance read: GNOME ELECTRONICS, A DIVISION OF THE KAWA COMPANY.

"Well, this is definitely the right place," James said.

"But the wrong entrance for us," IQ told him. "Look," he said, pointing to a series of wires. "This doorway has about a dozen alarms rigged to it. If we open the door or even touch the glass, they'll all go off."

James smiled. "But you can get around that, right?"

"Not so much around," IQ replied, "as over." He pointed to the gun in James's hand. "That pistol fires an incredibly strong, thin thread. The end of the thread has tiny barbs and will stick to anything—like the roof."

James aimed and pressed the trigger. He saw something metal flash by, and heard the thread on the reel whirring as it unwound. The end of the line seemed pretty well stuck to the roof. "Now what?" James asked.

"See this button on the side?" IQ explained. "When you press it, a small motor will draw in the thread. It may look flimsy, but I made it with space-age filament. It's strong enough to pull you up to the roof. Once you're there, press the button again to release the thread and toss the pistol down to me."

"Okay," James agreed. "Here goes nothing." He pressed the button. With a whine, the line tightened and the gun started to be tugged upward. Clutching it in both hands, James placed first one foot and then the other against the wall. As the line wound in he took a cautious step upward, bracing himself against the wall. Then he took another tentative step up the shiny surface. As the line continued to draw him up he was able to walk steadily up the outside of the glass wall. He reached the top and hoisted himself onto the edge of the roof. He pressed the button a second time. As soon as it rewound he threw the gun down to IQ.

IQ caught it and then started his climb. After he'd taken just a few steps, the motor in the gun started to make a funny noise, and sped up. The spool spun faster for a few seconds, then stopped abruptly. Just as IQ was trying to pull himself up hand over hand, the spool started to spin again. Then it spun faster and faster. Before IQ could stop the reel, his legs were tangled in the thread. In seconds he was completely tied up. The pistol kept reeling him in, and he was pulled, struggling, up to the roof. James grabbed the gun and hit the release button before the thread could tighten any more. Then he helped the young inventor out of the knots.

"I think that's one invention that needs a little more

work," James told him. "You looked like the catch of the day."

IQ hit the rewind button and the line retracted into the gun. He put it into his pocket with a frown. "Well, let's get on with it," he said, shaking his head over the failure of his invention.

James nodded and led the way to a skylight on the other side of the roof. They peered down through it and saw lights on in the room below. James could see a table, with several large chairs around it. A colorful graph was hanging on one wall of the room. On another were several bookcases and a long bar. "This looks like the boardroom," he whispered.

IQ knelt down. Using a small device he'd taken out of his pocket, he examined the skylight. "As I suspected," he said. "There's only one alarm. They aren't expecting visitors from above." He pulled a small suction cup on a wire from the top of the device and placed it over the corner of the glass. Then he surrounded the skylight with the wire. There was a small hook built into the top of the device, and IQ carefully hung it over the wire. Finally he activated the device and nodded with satisfaction.

"There we are," he told James. "I've interrupted the alarm circuit. As long as this is in place," he said, tapping the device, "we can open the glass without sounding the alarm."

Nodding, James pried open the skylight with his penknife. He trusted IQ, but as he'd just seen, sometimes the genius's inventions didn't work one hundred percent. This gadget, though, worked flaw-lessly. There was no alarm, and James dropped through the gap, landing softly on the table. IQ low-ered himself down beside James.

James looked around. There was a door at the end of the room, and he crossed to it. "Any alarms on this?" he asked.

IQ checked it out and then shook his head. James carefully eased open the door. It led into what looked like a secretary's office. There was a desk with a small computer, assorted stationery, and several trays filled with folders. Lining the walls were several large filing cabinets and a calendar of Japanese landscapes.

"I'll try the computer," IQ volunteered. "I may be able to find out something there."

"I doubt they're keeping Tracy in it," James replied dryly. "I'm going to take a look around."

IQ nodded. "Then you'd better take this," he sug-gested. He gave James a duplicate of the alarm de-tector he'd used on the skylight along with a few other devices. "This lights up when it senses an electronic alarm," he said, showing James. He also handed him the biosensor tracking device. It indicated that Tracy was still okay. "She must be around here," IQ ex-plained. "The sensor has a very limited range." Fi-nally he gave James the line-shooting gun. "It may be useful."

"Right," James replied softly. "You be careful. I'll be back soon." He checked the outer door of the secretary's office and slipped into the hall. With a bit of luck, he'd find Tracy without any trouble.

24

IQ settled down to investigate the computer files. This was the sort of thing he enjoyed and was good at. James was more than welcome to the action. When the computer came on, IQ happily began to check out the data. He didn't realize that by turning on the machine, he had set off a secret alarm deep in the heart of the building.

Chapter Four
Gnome Alone

James paused in the corridor. To the left was the entrance to another corridor; to the right, a set of stairs. If he were holding a prisoner, he thought, he'd either jail them at the top of the building or the bottom. Those would be the easiest spots to guard.

He had two choices, then: stay on the top floor, or go down.

He switched his special sunglasses to infrared, then ultraviolet, then back to normal. He didn't see any alarms. *Downstairs,* he decided silently. There'd most likely be alarms on the floor where they were holding Tracy captive.

He started to descend the stairs and noticed that the floor below had the same fluorescent lighting as the top floor. He wondered why there were even any lights on at this time of night. Just to make intruders think there were guards? Or because there really were guards? He stopped and then backtracked a few steps. Since there had been no alarms in the corridors, they were probably in use at night. Which meant that there would be people patrolling them.

So where were they?

James switched his sunglasses to infrared. As soon as he did he could see the heat from the bodies of two people who were crouched by the bottom of the stairs, waiting.

So they know someone's here, he said to himself. *We must have missed an alarm somewhere. Oh well.* The thing now was to get past the guards. Obviously, taking the stairs was out.

He pulled IQ's gun from his pocket and aimed it at the ceiling. It fired quietly, and the end of the line stuck to a metal crossbeam. James tucked his legs into his chest and swung over the railing of the stairs.

The two guards were taken completely by surprise as James cannonballed into them. They barely had time to look up before James rammed into them and sent them flying into each other. Their heads banged together, and they both looked stunned for a second. Then they tumbled, out cold, to the floor.

"Sleep well," James said. He was not at all surprised to see that they were dressed in the dark uniforms of S.C.U.M. agents.

James had encountered S.C.U.M. before. Saboteurs and Criminals United in Mayhem was an organization dedicated to crime and terrorism. If the evil group was responsible for the break-in at the museum,

James knew that whatever was going on was a lot more complicated than robbery—and more dangerous. And if S.C.U.M. had Tracy, James knew that he'd better find her before it was too late. For them, murder was nothing. In fact, S.C.U.M. agents had been known to kill just for the fun of it.

According to IQ's latest biosensor reading, Tracy was still apparently unharmed. Now all James had to do was find out where she was. James left the pistol hanging by its line in the stairwell. If more guards were on the alert, he might need it again.

He left the stairwell and found himself in another plushly carpeted corridor. James came to two doors in the middle of the corridor. He tested them with IQ's little device, but neither showed alarm systems. They probably didn't have anything worth investigating inside. At the end of the corridor he peered around the corner and quickly ducked back.

Just around the corner a guard was standing watch outside a door. He had a pistol in his hand and looked like a cross between a grizzly bear and a brick wall. He was protecting something—maybe Tracy.

James risked another quick look. Beyond the guard, on the other side of the door, was a tall potted tree. James pulled back his sleeve and took off his watch.

IQ had completely modified the watch. The emergency signal to his car was only one of its many functions. Another was a small missile launcher that had four tiny rockets. But right now James wanted something quieter—the laser. He aimed the watch at the base of the tree and fired. The beam quickly severed the trunk. There was a rustling noise as the leafy tree began to fall.

The guard jumped and started to turn around. Then he gave a cry as the tree collapsed on top of him. "Fall came early this year," James said, stepping over the unconscious body. Then he checked the door with IQ's alarm sensor. The light blinked like crazy. Copying what IQ had done on the roof, James attached the suction cup to one corner of the door. Then he made a loop of wire and clipped the device across the suction cup, completing the circuit. Having bypassed the alarm, he pushed the door open.

Except for the light leaking in from the corridor, it was dark inside. "Tracy?" he called quietly. "Are you here?"

He stepped forward. Something glittered on the floor. James bent down and picked it up. It was one of the biosensor earrings. It must have fallen from Tracy's ear. Or—was this a trap?

Suddenly, the room was flooded with light. Three Ninjas stood in the center of the floor. Their leader gave a low laugh.

"No, young Bond, she isn't here. But we are. Ninjas—attack!"

James was seeing spots because of the sudden light. He didn't stand a chance against the three assassins. "I guess I'd better *watch* out," he said and triggered the missile launcher in his wristwatch.

The four tiny rockets shot out and up. They hit the center of the ceiling and exploded. The Ninjas were showered in falling plaster and dust.

"Time to go," James decided. He turned and ran for the stairs. He could hear the assassins coming after him. It was going to be a close race! James rounded the corner and leaped into the stairwell. He grabbed the pistol and hit the rewind button.

He was just in time. The gun jerked him off his feet and up toward the ceiling. No sooner had his feet left the floor than two of the Ninjas collided as they tried to grab him.

"Going up," James said. "Third floor: computers and emergency exits."

The third Ninja had entered the stairwell. He couldn't reach James in time to stop him. Instead, he grabbed a throwing star from his belt and let it fly.

The spinning blades easily sliced through James's line. As he began to fall he let go of the gun and grabbed for the railing. His momentum carried him over the rail and he landed softly on the steps. He quickly ran the rest of the way back up to the top floor. As he raced down the corridor and back toward the boardroom he could hear the Ninjas gaining on him.

He threw open the door and skidded to a halt.

IQ wasn't alone. A fourth Ninja stood inside the room. The point of his sword was held to IQ's trembling neck.

Chapter Five
We're Out of Here!

"Sorry, James," IQ whispered, barely moving his lips. James could see the sword pushing into IQ's neck as he spoke.

The Ninja chuckled. "Surrender, young Bond," he called. "Or else . . ."

"I get the point," James agreed.

"I'm afraid I'm the one who'll get the point," IQ said bravely.

"You win," James told the Ninja. "For now, at least."

A second later the other three Ninjas burst through the door. When the leader saw IQ in the Ninja's grasp, he nodded. "You have done well," he told the guard. Then he looked at James, his eyes hard and cold. "You will come with us—for one final ride."

The Ninjas fell in around James and IQ and marched them off toward the stairs. IQ pushed his glasses back up his nose and gulped loudly.

"I'm glad that sword's no longer at my throat," he said. "But I think we're in some pretty serious trouble."

"Don't worry about it," James said lightly. He didn't want the Ninjas to know how scared he really was. "Did you find out anything before he caught you?"

"A little. Fat lot of good it'll do us now, though. Face it, James, we're goners."

"As Gordo would say—totally bogus, man!" James said.

As soon as he said Gordo's name James saw the flash of understanding in IQ's eyes. Then James silently triggered the alarm button on his watch. Now, if only Gordo was awake, they might have a chance.

"Silence," the leader of the Ninjas ordered. They were going down the stairs toward the main entrance. The Ninjas were hyper-alert. James knew they would get only one chance to make a break for it—if that.

James glanced through the glass wall as they approached the door. There was no sign at all of Gordo or the car. Desperately, he tapped the signal on

his watch again. Of all the times for Gordo to be napping . . .

A small gold plate was set in the wall by the main entrance. It was about four feet off the ground. The Ninja leader pulled the glove off his left hand and pressed his palm against the plate. The front door instantly slid open to allow them out. James and IQ had no choice but to move with the assassins.

Suddenly, they heard the squeal of rubber, and the small red sports car hurtled toward them. Gordo was hunched over the wheel, aiming the car right for the group. The Ninja guards took one look at the speeding vehicle and dove for cover.

As Gordo hit the brakes James could smell the tires burning. The car skidded around them in a tight circle. It slowed but didn't stop.

"Somebody need a ride?" Gordo yelled.

James grabbed IQ's arm and pushed him into the front seat of the car. Gordo started to pull away, and James vaulted into the back. As soon as James was in the car, Gordo floored the accelerator and roared away over the neatly cut lawn. IQ tried to sit up, but James reached forward and pushed him down again.

Four throwing stars whizzed through the air and slammed into the back of IQ's seat, missing James by only a few inches.

"Now I'll have to get the upholstery fixed," James said. "Darn!"

"It's a lot easier than getting *us* fixed!" IQ replied.

Gordo looked over his shoulder and steered the car away from Gnome Electronics. "And I thought I was going to miss all the fun," he said, grinning. "You wanna go back and do it again?"

"Thanks, Gordo," James replied. "But I've had enough excitement for one night."

"Totally bogus," Gordo said. James and IQ exchanged knowing glances as he flipped on the stereo, and they blasted back to Warfield.

The following morning James, Gordo and IQ met up with Phoebe Farragut in the school library. Phoebe was Tracy's roommate and best friend. They couldn't avoid telling Phoebe about Tracy's kidnapping. Right now, Phoebe's eyes burned with anger as James brought her up to date.

"So S.C.U.M. is behind all of this, James?" she asked, polishing her glasses with a handkerchief.

"It sure looks like it," he agreed. "Now they have Tracy—and the sword."

"I don't get it,"Gordo muttered. "There's all kinds of righteous stuff in the British Museum. Why go for some funky old sword?"

Phoebe glared at him. "It's not just *any* old sword— it's a special sword." She picked up the book she'd been studying. "It's known as the Sword of Death."

James picked up the book and looked for himself. There was a photo of the stolen sword. " 'From the Kamakura period,' " he read. " 'The *shogun*'s sword, fashioned from the metal of a meteorite.' "

"A meteorite?" Gordo repeated. "Wild!"

"Does that mean they didn't have the technology to extract iron ore from the earth?" Phoebe asked.

"In twelfth-century Japan they were quite capable of mining iron," James said thoughtfully. "So the fact that the metal came from a meteorite must have some kind of significance."

Phoebe shrugged. "It may have been symbolic,"

she suggested. "You know, like the gods are on your side. According to this book, the sword had magic powers and helped Minamoto Yoritomo, the sword's owner, rise to power."

"Awesome!" Gordo said. "Just like Excalibur and that King Arthur dude."

James shook his head. "This is all very fascinating, but it doesn't explain why S.C.U.M. wanted the sword badly enough to steal it in broad daylight. Or why they took Tracy hostage." He spread his hands. "We've seen S.C.U.M.'s work before. This hardly seems to be their sort of thing. For them, stealing a sword is minor stuff. If they hadn't kidnapped Tracy, I'd just have left it to the police."

"Especially now that the sword is no longer in England," IQ added. "From my . . . uh . . . research last night, I found that it has been taken to Tokyo. That's where the Kawa Company has its headquarters."

"And that's probably where we'll find Tracy," James said. "But I'd be happier if we knew what was so valuable about this sword."

IQ pulled out the artificial rose he'd been wearing off and on for the past day or so. "This may hold the answer," he said proudly.

"A rose?" Phoebe asked.

Gordo laughed. "Dude! I didn't know you were a buttonist."

"That's *botanist*," Phoebe corrected him.

"Oh yeah?" Gordo asked. "So how come he's been wearing it in his *button*hole?"

IQ held the rose out for them to see. "If you examine it closely, you'll see that it's actually a fake." He pressed one of the thorns on the stem, and the petals opened outward. In the center was a tiny lens. "It's my latest invention—a microcamera. I wore it to the British Museum yesterday."

"IQ!" Phoebe said disapprovingly. "How could you? You know cameras aren't allowed in the British Museum!"

"Well, that's the whole point," he answered, looking a little red-faced. "In order to test it as an undercover camera, I had to try it in a place where cameras aren't allowed. There's no point in using it for taking snapshots."

"Don't worry about it, IQ," James said. "We won't turn you in—if the pictures help us figure out what's going on."

Back in the dorm room IQ and James shared, the four of them examined the pictures. Phoebe shuddered when she saw the Ninjas.

"Tall, dark, and gruesome," she muttered. "I'm glad I missed that trip."

Gordo tossed down the pictures he'd been studying. "It looks like stuff from a bad kung fu flick," he complained. "There's nothing useful here."

"I'm not so sure," James said, examining one of the shots carefully. It showed the hand of a Ninja as he pulled the sword from the mannequin's grip. "IQ, could you blow up this shot? I want to get a better look at the hilt of the sword."

IQ nodded. "Give me a minute or two."

"While you're at it," Gordo added, "I'd like a half-dozen wallet size." Phoebe gave him a withering look.

IQ disappeared into the bathroom, where he'd temporarily set up a darkroom.

"Did you see something that will help save Tracy?" Phoebe asked James.

"I'm not sure," he told her. "Do you still have that book you were looking at in the library?" Phoebe always carried a huge bag over her shoulder. She said it had to be big enough to hold anything she might decide to buy. That was sort of a joke, but not really. Phoebe's father was incredibly rich. He also usually let Phoebe have whatever she wanted. She had an enormous allowance plus unlimited credit cards and her own checking account.

Now she dug through the bag and pulled out the red book.

"*Ancient Japan,* by Professor Tetsuru Tanaka," James said, reading the book's spine. "Good choice; it's one of the classics in the field. Now, where's that picture of the sword?" He found the page and showed the photo to Phoebe and Gordo. "The hilt has something carved into it. This picture's too tiny to show us what, but if IQ can get us a clear enlarged image, we might be able to see more."

"Got it!" IQ called. He came out of the bathroom and handed the picture to James.

About half of the handle was clearly visible. Figures and shapes were cut into the ivory, but James had no idea what they meant.

"It looks like a map!" Phoebe said, pointing. "Those must be the four main islands of Japan."

"You're right, Phoebe," James agreed. "And it might mean something if we knew what the text says."

"I've got that covered, no prob," Gordo replied. "My dad's a mega-master with codes. I'll bet he could work it out easy."

James smiled. "He might be able to—if this were a code. But it isn't—it's an ancient Japanese script. I can read *modern* Japanese, but there are probably only a few scholars in the world who could decipher this inscription."

Phoebe tapped the book. "I'll bet that Professor Tanaka could read it for us."

"Most excellent notion," Gordo agreed.

"Only, according to the author's bio," Phoebe added, "he lives in Japan."

Chapter Six
Destination: Tokyo

"It's starting to make some sense," James said. He was with IQ and Gordo in the boys' locker room. James was almost happy about the track tryouts Mr. Mitchell was holding that day. It took his mind off Tracy, even if only for a moment. "Everything points to Japan."

"Tokyo, to be exact," IQ agreed. "That's where Kawa has its headquarters. It's where the stolen sword was shipped. It's where Professor Tanaka lives." He pulled on his running shoes. "And where Tracy is no doubt a prisoner."

"Right," James agreed. "So we've got to get to Japan somehow."

"Don't look at me, dude," Gordo said. "I already spent my allowance."

"Phoebe can probably help," IQ suggested. "One

of the companies that her father owns is an air cargo firm."

"Tokyo, here we come," Gordo said. "High-tech electronics. Great food. Godzilla."

He broke off as a head suddenly poked around the nearest locker. Trevor Noseworthy grinned nastily at Gordo. "Planning to play hooky and sneak off to Japan, eh?"

"You were spying on us!" IQ exclaimed.

"Of course I was," Trevor agreed. "How else would I know what to tell Mr. Milbanks?"

Gordo stood up and glared down at Trevor. "Don't even think about it, toad!"

Trevor stuck out his tongue. "Try and stop me." He turned around and ran for the door before Gordo could get into motion. But he didn't make it out of the door. Instead, he smacked right into Mr. Mitchell.

"While I admire your enthusiasm to get running, Noseworthy," the gym teacher said with a frown, "the track is in the other direction."

"But I was going to see Mr. Milbanks, sir," Trevor started to explain.

"I'm sure it can wait until *after* track," Mr. Mitchell replied.

Trevor looked unhappy about the delay but turned back to the locker room. "Oh, I suppose so." But when he saw the dejected looks on Gordo, IQ, and James's faces, he cheered up again. "You'll soon be in detention!" he sneered as he ran out toward the track.

"Come on, guys—you, too," Mr. Mitchell said, giving them a speculative look. "See you outside."

When Mr. Mitchell had left for the field, IQ turned urgently to James. "If Trevor tells Milbanks, we're done for."

"Not if I get my hands on the little creep first," Gordo snarled, twisting his hands around an imaginary neck.

"Effective but crude, Gordo," James said. "I have a simpler plan." He crossed to the wall, where there was a sheet pinned to the bulletin board. "There's a cross-country practice this afternoon."

"Are you going to volunteer?" asked IQ, puzzled.

James took the pencil. "Yes—but not myself." He scrawled a good imitation of Trevor's signature on the form. "Didn't you see how much Trevor enjoyed running? I'm sure he'll appreciate this."

"I know I will." Gordo grinned.

James had trouble concentrating on the track as he ran. His thoughts kept going to Tracy. Was she still okay? Would they be able to save her? What was she going through right now?

As James crashed into a hurdle he could hear Trevor's nasty laugh. "What's wrong, Bond?" he sneered. "Worried about what old Milbanks will do when I tell him what you're up to?"

"This doesn't seem to be your day, James." Mr. Mitchell cut James off before he could answer Trevor's annoying question. "Well, maybe you'll do better with the hurdles next time. You guys go hit the showers." As Trevor started off, though, the gym teacher grabbed his shoulder. "Not you, Noseworthy. You signed up for cross-country, remember?"

"Me?" Trevor squeaked. "But . . . I mean, I didn't—"

"I like to see you getting so involved in sports," Mr. Mitchell went on, ignoring Trevor's protests. "It shows good school spirit. And today's run is really easy. It's just eight miles."

"Eight *miles?*" Trevor echoed. He looked like he was about to faint.

"Nothing to it." The teacher grinned. "Come on, I'll even go part of the way with you. Get those legs moving!"

Trevor turned back to glare at James and the others. "You did this, Bond! I'll get you for this!"

"Save your breath, Trevor," James suggested. "I've got a feeling you're going to need it!"

A short while later James pulled up to the main security fence that surrounded Warfield Academy. He was driving the academy's van. The guard peered in through the window. Aside from James, the only thing visible was a large wooden crate.

"Let's see your pass," the guard said. James handed it over and held his breath. IQ had promised his forgery was undetectable. This was the moment of truth.

The guard handed it back. "What's in the box?" he asked.

"Broken gym equipment," James replied. "Mr. Mitchell is having it shipped back. I've got to drop it off at the station."

Nodding, the guard waved him through. James drove on carefully. When he was certain they were out of sight of the school, he stopped the van and opened the crate.

Phoebe, IQ, and Gordo piled out, stretching their cramped limbs. Phoebe glared at IQ.

"Next time," she said, "you make the pass in *my* name."

IQ straightened his glasses and nodded sheepishly, then started pulling out their bags. Each of them had packed a couple of changes of clothes, and IQ had brought along a few "essentials" to help out. He checked to make sure that they had everything they needed.

"You still have the sunglasses, don't you, James?" he asked.

"In my pocket," James replied. "I thought they'd come in handy. No offense, IQ," he added, "but I hope you didn't bring the line-firing gun this time. I think it still needs a little work on the winding reel."

"Something better," IQ assured him. "I've packed my collapsible mini crossbow. Wait till you see this one in action!"

James nodded. "Phoebe, you're sure that you've got us reservations to Tokyo?"

"Relax, James," she replied. "It's all set up. Trust me."

A huge 747 luxury jet sliced through the skies toward the Japanese islands. On board, passengers were being served their meals. Some relaxed while watching the in-flight movie. All were comfortable on the long flight.

A few thousand feet below the jumbo jet, an older cargo plane cut into the clouds. Inside it, Gordo was glaring out of the window at the 747. "I've always wanted to visit Japan," he said. "But not as *baggage*."

James glanced at his friend and tried not to laugh. The aircraft they were in was far from luxurious. It was filled with boxes, suitcases, and crates. There were just a few old and worn-out seats. Gordo was sharing his with a small terrier in a shipping crate. The puppy leaned out and licked Gordo's face. Rubbing the wet spot, Gordo moved as far away from the dog as he could.

"Relax, Gordo," James advised.

"I wish I could," Gordo grumbled. "But I feel like a windshield in a rainstorm." He glared at the puppy. "Cut it out, okay?" The dog licked his hand, the only part of Gordo he could reach.

Phoebe, annoyed by Gordo's criticism, pointed to the emergency exit. "Maybe you'd like to get out and walk?"

Gordo threw up his hands. "Forget I said anything," he replied. He sat back in his seat next to the dog, who immediately began licking his face again. "It's a long way to Tokyo," he sighed.

Chapter Seven
Tanaka's World

Tokyo was a huge, busy city, with tall buildings of glass and steel. Flashing neon signs were everywhere, and the streets were lined with shops. Some of the people rushing around wore business suits and Western-style clothing; others wore more traditional Japanese garb.

Phoebe stopped to stare into a store window. It was filled with stereo equipment and hundreds of compact discs, all labeled in both Japanese and English. "I could spend hours shopping here," she said with a sigh. Then she turned her back on the window. "But we've got more important things to do."

"Right," James agreed. He checked the guidebook he'd picked up at the airport. "Professor Tanaka works at the Japanese National Museum, and according to this map, we're almost there."

In a few minutes they arrived at the main entrance to the modern-looking museum. A flight of wide steps led up to the black glass walls at the front of the building.

"Here we are," James said. "I'd better talk to the Professor alone. Why don't you guys find our hotel and then see what you can dig up about this Kawa Company? Like an address, owners—that sort of thing."

"Gotcha," Gordo agreed. "Catch you later."

James entered the museum and asked for directions to Professor Tanaka's office. He found his way, and knocked on the door. A woman's voice invited him in.

She was pretty and about the same age as James. Her straight jet-black hair shone in the light as she looked up from her notepad. She flashed James a friendly smile.

Long, overloaded shelves filled most of the room. There were many artifacts on the shelves—weapons, armor, bowls, porcelain, teacups, screens, paintings, and books. It looked like this young woman was cataloguing the items. They were probably new additions to the collection.

"Ah—I'm looking for Professor Tanaka," James said. "I'm sorry to disturb you, but it's quite urgent that I see him."

The girl shook her head slightly. "I'm sorry, but the Professor is not here at the moment, Mr., um . . ." She looked at him questioningly.

"Bond," he told her. "James Bond Jr. I don't mind waiting. I can admire the . . . scenery." He flashed her a smile.

Her eyes sparkled. "Then I'm afraid you will have quite a long wait. Professor Tanaka always spends a portion of his afternoons meditating at the local Buddhist temple." She indicated a small photo on the desk. It showed an elderly, white-haired man who was wearing a robe. He was sitting cross-legged in a small temple. "Perhaps I can help you?"

"I wish you could," James sighed. "But I doubt it." He showed her IQ's photo of the sword hilt. "Unless you can decipher this inscription."

She examined the picture and her eyes opened wide. "That is the Yoritomo sword!"

"You know your history," James said.

"We heard the sword had been stolen while it was on loan in London," the secretary said. "What do you know of this sword?"

"I don't know where it is," James told her. "But I think I know who stole it."

She began scribbling on her notepad. She tore off a piece of paper and handed it to James. "This is where you will find Professor Tanaka. I wish you well in your quest."

"Thank you," James said. "You've been more than helpful." He smiled again and left the office.

The young girl stared thoughtfully at the door. Then she put away her pad and pen. She crossed the room to a small closet and opened its door. A black

Ninja outfit and its matching mask were hanging inside. She quickly pulled it on and then slipped out of the office after James.

Every muscle in Trevor's body ached from running the eight-mile course. Actually, he'd stumbled more than he'd run for the last six miles! He flopped down on one of the benches in the locker room and gave a long, deep sigh.

Then he remembered about Bond and the others. Wearily, he managed to sit up. He had to fix that Bond! If only he had the energy to do it. He could barely muster the strength to lift his wrist and see what time it was.

The door opened, and Mr. Mitchell came over to the bench. "It's about time," he said. "I'm glad to see you completed the course, Trevor. I didn't think you had it in you."

"It isn't in me anymore," Trevor said, yawning. "But I've got to talk to Mr. Milbanks."

"Of course," Mr. Mitchell agreed. "But you look absolutely exhausted. You ran a long, long way today . . . and tonight."

"Well," Trevor said, still panting. "I *am* tired . . ."

"That's right, Trevor," the gym teacher said. "Take a short rest. Just a little sleep. Sleep . . . sleep . . ."

Trevor fell back on the bench and his muscles began to relax. His eyes closed, and within seconds he was snoring away. Mr. Mitchell tiptoed out of the room. He'd helped James all he could for now.

James had traveled to the small park that held the Buddhist temple. A small stream flowed past the gateway. James crossed the tiny bridge, amazed at how quiet and peaceful it seemed here. Only a few hundred yards away, the city was a noisy hive of activity. He could see why Professor Tanaka would come here to meditate each day.

James paused and removed his shoes at the entrance to the temple. Then he walked through the two upright posts that marked the entrance. Inside, the walls were made of sliding rice-paper screens. The floors were brightly polished cherry wood.

James spotted a man sitting in one of the several tiny rooms. His head was slightly bowed as he meditated in front of a low wood altar. James recognized the man from the photo in the museum office. Entering the room, James said softly, "Professor Tanaka?"

The man raised his eyes, and then stood up. He bowed to the altar, then turned to James. "Yes, I am Professor Tanaka."

"My name is Bond," James told him. "James Bond Jr. I'm sorry to disturb you, but it is urgent that I speak with you, Professor."

The old man inclined his head slightly. "So," he said formally. He pointed at James's sock-clad feet. "I am pleased to see that a young man such as yourself honors our customs."

"Where honor is due," James answered, "then it is a pleasure to give it."

Professor Tanaka smiled. "A good reply. Now, how may I be of service to you, Bond-san?"

Before James could reply, the paper screen behind the Professor slid open. Two men dressed in the black outfits of Ninja assassins grabbed the Professor. With a startled cry, he was jerked backward off his feet and pulled out of the room.

Chapter Eight
Down and Out

The last place James would have expected trouble was in the temple. "It's not even safe to meditate anymore," he muttered. Then he leaped across the room and threw himself at the paper screen.

It tore as he burst through to the other side. The room he found himself in was almost identical to the previous one. Only this room had a door to the outside, which was now open. James rushed out and saw that the two Ninjas had been prepared for a quick getaway. There was a motorcycle with its engine running. It had a sidecar, into which the two men stuffed the struggling Professor. As one of the Ninjas jumped onto the bike, the other turned, drawing his throwing stars.

James dove for cover behind a giant gong that stood next to the exit. As the first Ninja roared away with the Professor, the second ran toward James. Leaping into the air feet first, James hit the gong with all of his strength. It swung back and smacked the startled Ninja right in the face. The metal rang loudly from the impact.

James raced around the swinging gong and jumped over the fallen Ninja. He could barely see the motorcycle as it wove through the Tokyo traffic. He looked around quickly and spotted a bicycle leaning against a nearby tree. Ignoring the protesting yell of its owner, James hopped onto the bike and started down the path.

He didn't get far. Two policemen were standing by the entrance to the park. As James drew level with them they both reached out and grabbed him.

"The police," James groaned. "Just the people I wanted to see."

One of the policemen snapped a pair of handcuffs on James's wrists while the other yanked him off the bike. As he was led to their waiting car, James saw the motorcycle vanishing into a side street.

The Professor was gone. And so was James's best chance at finding a clue to Tracy's captors.

Finally, the police were done interviewing all the witnesses. They knew James had been trying to save the Professor, not steal a bicycle. They let him go. James made his way to the hotel where Phoebe had booked them rooms. He arrived at the hotel's restaurant with a long face.

"Cheer up, James," Phoebe said. "It could have been worse."

James shook his head and stared at his plate. "I don't see how much worse things could be," he replied. "Those S.C.U.M. Ninjas took Professor Tanaka before I had a chance to speak to him. Then the police arrested me for stealing a bike. And by the time they'd verified my story, the Ninja I'd knocked out was already gone. Now we're back at square one—in Japan, with no leads, no Professor, and no sign of Tracy." He looked at Gordo and IQ. "Did you guys have any better luck?"

"Yeah," Gordo replied, staring across the room as the waitress arrived with their order. "We found this truly excellent place to eat. And check out our waitress."

James looked at the girl without much interest. She was dressed in the traditional *geisha* style, with a long, flowing robe. Her dark hair was knotted on top of her head and held in place by wooden sticks. Her face was powdered to a pale shade, and her eyes and lips were carefully made up. Despite the costume, there was something familiar about her.

Gordo studied the meal she set before him. It looked like raw fish. "Hey!" he said, "I wanted mine well done."

"You ordered *sashimi,* Gordo," IQ said. "It's sliced fish. That's ginger and seaweed." IQ pointed at the plate. "That's soy sauce and *wasabi*—a very spicy horseradish."

"It's all fish. *Raw* fish," Gordo grumbled. He looked at the waitress. "Do we get a discount because they forgot to cook it?"

"Gordo!" Phoebe said in horror. "It's *supposed* to be uncooked!"

IQ stared at Gordo's plate and shuddered. "I like my fish *fresh*—but not raw." The waitress knelt down beside the table. In the center was a large iron pot over a low flame. She began to cook the rest of the meal inside it. "*Sukiyaki!*" IQ said happily. "Beef and vegetables cooked right at the table."

James sighed. "It's hard to concentrate on food, IQ," he said. "I've let Tracy down." He glanced once again at the biosensor. It indicated that Tracy was at least still alive. "If only we could find out something about this Kawa Company."

The hostess gave him a smile and a low bow. "Permit me to help you," she suggested. "I know the firm you seek. They manufacture electronics. There is a rumor that they are owned by the Yakuza."

"Gesundheit," Gordo said, trying a little of his *sashimi.* "Hey, this is mucho tasty."

"The Yakuza is a Japanese organization dedicated to crime, Gordo," James explained. He looked at the waitress. "Can you tell me where the Kawa Company is located? It's very important that I find them."

"In the business sector," the girl replied. "I will get you their address when you have finished eating."

"Thank you," James said. "You've been a big help." He turned to IQ. "I hope that your gadgets are all ready."

IQ smiled. "I think you'll find them very handy for whatever you're planning."

"Oh, I expect I'll just hang out and see what comes from it."

The waitress studied him, her face unreadable. "If the Yakuza are truly the owners of the firm," she told him, "you could be in very grave danger. Their usual remedy for trespassers is to kill them."

Chapter Nine
Tracy in Trouble

Tracy Milbanks did not scare easily. She was scared stiff right now.

She'd been kidnapped by Ninjas, smuggled out of England to Japan, and held prisoner in a small, dark room. Masked men and women had fed her and given her clean clothes. She was watched by a tall, silent female guard at all times, but she hadn't been hurt.

Until now.

Six Ninja commandos and their leader had piled into the room. Two of them firmly held her wrists against the arms of the chair in which she was seated. Two more held an elderly Japanese man. The remaining Ninjas stood back and guarded the door.

The elderly man sat across from Tracy at a large table. He looked both frightened and furious. He had refused to answer any of the questions that the Ninja leader had asked him. Now, though, the questioner had lost his patience.

"Enough!" he thundered. He reached over his shoulder and pulled a gleaming sword from its sheath across his back. "Professor, you are wasting our time. If words do not persuade you, then I shall resort to action."

He glanced down at the table. There was a telephone on it, but nothing else. His eyes seemed to bore into the phone. Then, with a yell that made Tracy jump out of her seat, he swung the sword up and then down in a short arc. The blade slashed into the telephone, severing it neatly in half. The Ninja leader pushed the two pieces apart.

"Observe," he said darkly, "what my sword will do. Now . . ." He nodded his head to the guard on Tracy's left. Tracy gave a cry of pain as the Ninja pulled her hand forward. Holding Tracy's hand by the wrist, the guard forced her to lay her palm on the tabletop.

The leader stepped around the table. His eyes narrowed. "I knew that we would find a use for the American girl." He looked at Professor Tanaka. "Now, imagine what my sword will do to her hand!" He brought his weapon around in a swinging arc.

Tracy screamed in terror. She tried to pull her arm out of the way, but the guards were too strong. She closed her eyes tightly, held her breath, and waited for the pain.

"No!" cried the Professor. "Don't!"

At the last possible moment, the leader's hand twisted slightly. The tip of his sword sank into the

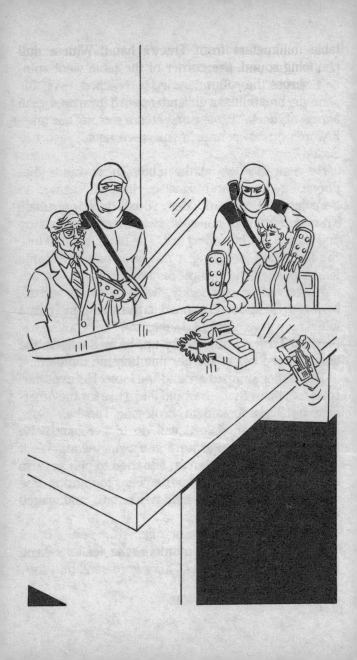

table millimeters from Tracy's hand. With a dull chopping sound, the corner of the table went spinning across the room.

Tracy breathed again and opened her eyes. She almost fainted when she saw that a piece of the table just in front of her fingernails was missing.

The Ninja leader looked at the Professor again. "Well?" he growled. "Will you help us? I promise that my next blow will not miss."

Professor Tanaka nodded. "I will do as you ask," he said in a shaky voice. "But spare the young lady any further suffering."

The Ninja barked a laugh. "That's not up to me, Professor—it's up to you! As long as you cooperate fully, she is safe. But if you lie to us or try to stop us—then I will serve you her fingers on a plate."

When Trevor finally woke up, he was astonished to discover that bright morning light was streaming in through the locker room windows. He must have slept on the bench all night!

He straightened out with a groan as pain shot through his aching muscles. His pillow had been some dirty team uniforms. It had been the first night in his life that he had slept on anything but goose-down pillows.

"I'm going to ache all day," he muttered to himself. "And it's all that Bond's fault."

Bond . . . There was something about James Bond that he'd been meaning to do before he dozed off. What was it?

"Japan!" he exclaimed. "That's it! Japan . . ." He climbed stiffly to his feet, trying to ignore all of the aches and pains in his tortured body. He had to tell the headmaster his news.

James stood on the roof of the high-rise apartment building and stared out across the night sky. He could see the flashing neon signs of tourist spots, night-clubs, and restaurants on the ground hundreds of feet below.

Facing him was a wall of blackness—the Kawa Company building. Made of black glass, it was impossible to see into the building from the outside. On the roof, a neon sign with a huge letter K glowed green in the dark sky.

"I always wanted to get to the top in business," James said to himself. "Now's the time to do it." He put down the small backpack he was carrying and took out IQ's collapsible mini crossbow. James pulled back the string until it locked into firing position over the trigger, then took from his pack one of the bolts the bow fired. It was a small metal arrow with a razor-sharp tip. The end of the bolt was attached to a spool of IQ's thin, superstrong rope. James loaded the bow and then aimed for the base of the neon sign. A gentle pull on the trigger sent the bolt flying through the sky. With a soft *thunk*, the arrow buried itself in the sign.

James dropped the bow and tested the rope. It seemed to be well anchored; he just hoped it would hold his weight. He tied the end of the rope around the leg of the huge water tower on the apartment house roof. The rope was now stretched tightly between the two buildings, almost two hundred feet above the street.

"Uncle James has done this dozens of times," he told himself as he stood on the edge of the roof. He carefully put one foot out on the rope. "Or so he says . . ." The rope stayed taut. Now came the tricky part—the second foot.

He slowly took one step after another, his arms stretched wide for balance. The rope sagged a little, swaying sickeningly as he moved across the gap between the buildings. Far, far below were the lights of the night traffic.

Suddenly his foot slipped! Trying not to fall, he overbalanced. His arms windmilled as he tried to regain his footing on the swaying rope.

Then he fell.

As he dropped he managed to grab the rope with his right hand. There was a sharp pain in his shoulder, but his grip held. He dangled by one hand nearly two hundred feet in the air. Still, he was relieved that he'd hit the rope instead of the ground.

"Uncle James can do it his way," he muttered under his breath. "I'll do it mine."

He started forward again, swinging from hand to hand. It was much easier—and safer—for him this way.

On the roof he had just left, a figure in a Ninja costume stepped out of the shadows. A knife flashed in the Ninja's hand. With one quick flick of the wrist,

James's rope was severed. *"Sayonara,"* the Ninja whispered into the night.

With a startled cry, James tightened his grip on the rope as he swung toward the sheer wall of the Kawa Building. He searched wildly for an open window—or anything he could aim for—but the wall was unbroken.

In just a few seconds, he'd discover what it felt like to be a bug hitting a car window at high speed.

Chapter Ten
Sword Play

Just as James was about to hit the wall, a small opening appeared. It was not unlike the eye of a camera lens. James realized that steel shutters in the wall were opening up silently. The opening was just large enough for him to zoom through. James breathed a fervent prayer of thanks.

He let go of the rope and landed on the floor of a large, dark room. He slid across the highly polished black floor until he banged into something soft. As James caught his breath he realized that what he'd hit was a tall, padded chair. Come to think of it, he was feeling pretty shaky after his high-wire ordeal. Gratefully, he sank back against the chair's soft, soft cushions.

"Now this is real Japanese hospitality!" he said in relief. Then, before he could move, clamps snapped around his chest, arms, and legs, pinning him to the chair. "But *this* isn't," he sighed.

The overhead lights suddenly came on. The room was huge and nearly empty. James could still see the skyline of Tokyo through the gap in the wall. A sleek black helicopter stood close to the opening. Obviously the shuttered entrance was for launching the copter. He'd been very lucky to hit that spot, that was for sure!

A Japanese box kite hung from the wall next to the helicopter. Three black hang gliders were suspended by ropes from the ceiling. All along the walls were cases filled with laser weapons.

James looked across the steel table that stood directly in front of him. On the other side of the table was a large, thronelike chair. In the chair, watching James with burning yellow eyes, was a man dressed in a red and purple outfit that clung to his muscular body. The shoulders of the outfit were so built up that they jutted out like wings. The black outline of a dragon was sewn across the chest. The man had long gray hair, and the ends of his thin mustache hung like tusks down to his chest. He was definitely weird-looking. But there was one thing about him that made him downright bizarre—and terrifying.

Both of his hands were made completely out of metal. James could see joints in the steel fingers and wrists, and the bionic hands even had bladelike metal fingernails. He could imagine the force that they could produce if the fingers were closed over, say, his own hand. His fingers would be crushed in a second. Better not offer to shake hands with the mutant, then.

"Welcome to Japan, young Bond," the man said. "Like your uncle, you enjoy making a colorful entrance, I see."

James noticed that there were two items on the table in front of the man. Both were swords, and one of them he recognized.

"The Yoritomo sword!" James said. "So you're the one who stole it!"

The man shrugged. "Let us just say that my loyal Ninjas appropriated it—despite the petty interference you caused." He stood up, and James could see that he was well over six feet tall. "But I am not being a good host. Permit me to introduce myself. I am Dr. No."

"Dr. No!" James stared at him in astonishment. "My uncle told me all about you. But he said you were dead!"

Dr. No smiled. It was an ugly sight. He had the smile of a shark about to strike. "The whole world thought I was dead. But, as you see, it is far from true. I am indeed very much alive."

James was puzzled. Uncle James had told him that Dr. No had once tried to start World War III. "Stealing museum artifacts is hardly your line, is it? Or have you decided to stick to smaller crimes from now on? What are you planning next? A gas station holdup?"

Dr. No shook his head once, carefully. "My plans remain as they always have been—complete world domination."

67

"That's a pretty tall order for someone with two small swords," James jeered.

Dr. No picked up the stolen sword and walked around to stand in front of James. Then, he swiftly slashed out with the sword. For an instant, James expected to be stabbed through the chest. Then the blow was over. The sword had cut the metal bands around his chest. It had also sliced through his jacket and shirt and nicked his skin.

"I think you've made your point," he said. The bands around his wrists and ankles still held him prisoner.

"Not yet," Dr. No replied. "I wouldn't want you to think I am only a petty thief. Please pay careful attention."

A door at the far end of the room opened, and three of Dr. No's Ninjas entered. They bowed to Dr. No and moved silently across the room. One stood on either side of James and the third went over to one of the cabinets containing the laser guns. He unlocked it and brought the largest gun to the table.

Dr. No turned back to face James. "Over the years I have secretly built up the Kawa Company. It makes many harmless items intended for the amusement of the masses—stereo components, video games, and the like. But it also produces other items solely for my own private use." He picked up the laser rifle and tapped a code into a small panel on the weapon. It began to hum quietly. "The power of light has always fascinated me. When lasers were first invented in the late nineteen-fifties, there was much talk of their becoming the death rays of the comic books. Yet, thirty-five years later, we still don't see them used in the war zones of the world. You seem to be well educated, young Bond—can you tell me why lasers are not the ray guns people once thought they would be?"

James shrugged. "It's a matter of power," he said. "Lasers need a lot of it. There's no generator small and economical enough to make lasers practical weapons. Lasers are used only by doctors and to play compact discs and scan prices in supermarkets." He glanced at the rifle in front of him. "And by S.C.U.M. agents, to knock people out."

Dr. No smiled. "Quite right—until now." He turned the laser rifle around and pointed it directly at James.

"You haven't been boring me, Dr. No," he said as cheerfully as he could. "Please don't start now."

Dr. No lifted the laser up, aimed, and fired.

The clamps holding James's legs glowed red, then split apart. Then Dr. No did the same to the clamps holding James's wrists. As they clattered to the floor Dr. No put the laser rifle back on the table. James stood up, and the two Ninjas held him by the upper arms next to the chair.

"That's the most powerful laser rifle available," Dr. No continued. "But after three or four shots, it takes several hours to recharge. As you say, not enough power. However . . ." He picked up the stolen sword and stabbed it into the metal table. "My scientists discovered something very interesting. It seems that there are some very rare forms of meteorites that contain a previously unknown isotope of iron. This isotope—a variation of normal iron—has unique properties." He pointed to the second sword, which was still lying flat on the table.

"That is the partner to the Yoritomo sword. All samurai warriors used two blades, one large and one small. The small one I . . . *obtained* shall we say, from a museum collection in Japan. My scientists experimented with the sword, and we found that it has the ability to amplify any force a hundredfold!"

He snatched up the laser gun again and aimed it at the blade of the Yoritomo sword. He pulled the trigger. James could see the red beam as it left the rifle. It hit the sword and reflected off the blade onto the chair by his side.

The chair started to melt and then vanished in a bright, soundless explosion.

Dr. No burst into laughter at the frightened expression on James's face.

"As you can see, a much more interesting weapon." He threw aside the laser gun and pulled the sword from the table. He turned back to James, waving the sword through the air. One metal claw tapped the carved ivory on the handle.

"The first sword I stole proved that the Yoritomo sword contained the right isotope, but I did not know where the meteorite it was made from was hidden. This map is all that I needed. According to the legend, the meteorite weighs several tons. Once I find it, I shall be able to annihilate any army in the world with only a dozen men. With that meteorite in my possession, I shall be able to rule the world!"

"I've heard plenty of people make claims like that," James said with a laugh. "Most of them are now wearing straitjackets. Anyway, I've seen that map. It's in ancient Japanese—and I doubt it's a tongue you're very fluent in."

"You're quite correct," Dr. No admitted. "But, once again, just a little out of date. I know that you tried to see Professor Tanaka—my Ninjas reported this to me when they kidnapped him. He is now my prisoner—along with that pretty friend of yours."

"Tracy!" James glared fiercely at his captor. "Where is she?"

"She is intact." Dr. No smiled again. "Professor Tanaka was very helpful. By translating the map for me, he saved Miss Milbanks's fingers for her. I would have let the girl go, but I may need more help from the Professor. As we speak they are on their way to O-Shima." He nodded to his Ninjas, who tightened their grips around James's arms. "Meanwhile, I believe you were falling to your death. This has been a pleasant interlude, but there's no denying the gravity of the situation." He looked at his men. "Take him to the exit and throw him out. When his body is found, the police will no doubt assume he was involved in some foolhardy stunt and slipped." Again, he gave James his chilly, evil smile. "Bye-bye, Bond."

Chapter Eleven
Night Flight

James struggled as the two men dragged him toward the opening in the outer wall. He was unable to break free; both men were extremely strong. At the edge of the room, James looked out. He could see the road below—with a couple of hundred feet of empty space between it and his body. Then a sudden movement on the roof of the next building caught his eye.

A black-clad figure raised IQ's mini crossbow and fired just as the Ninjas were about to throw James through the opening.

The arrow missed the Ninja on James's left by about an inch. He jumped back from the edge, letting go of James in his shock. James took advantage of the break. He had studied martial arts himself. With his free hand, he punched the other Ninja with a karate blow. That man groaned and clutched his stomach. James was free. He quickly glanced across the way, seeing his mysterious rescuer duck back into the shadows.

"It looks like I have friends in high places," he commented to himself. Before the two Ninja guards could recover, James dashed back into the room. He headed for the cabinets that held the laser guns—with three Ninjas and Dr. No to fight, he'd need a lot of help! But the Ninja with Dr. No realized what James was doing and moved to intercept him.

"There's no escape!" Dr. No yelled furiously. "You're going out of that door!"

"Thanks for the suggestion," James said, changing his course. He had reached the wall where the huge kite hung. Snatching it from its hooks, he spun around and ran back toward the opening.

The two Ninjas weren't expecting this move. They thought James would try to escape in the other direction. Instead, he plowed through them and flung himself out of the hole in the wall, hanging onto one of the kite's crossbars.

The Ninjas and Dr. No dashed across to the opening and looked out.

As soon as James was out of the building, he wondered if he'd made a colossal mistake. He was dropping like a brick. Still, what other choice did he have? Then his plunge toward the pavement seemed to slow. The updrafts of warm air from the ground caught the kite, and it started to soar.

"Going up!" James said with relief.

Dr. No glared at the escaping kite. Then he spun around to face his Ninjas. "Don't just stand there!" he howled. "Young Bond knows our plans now. Stop him, you fools!" He pointed to the hang gliders. "Quickly, you idiots!"

At that moment James was feeling pretty good. He'd escaped from the clutches of Dr. No, and it seemed as if he had an unknown ally. And he'd discovered that Tracy was alive and on her way to O-Shima. He had no idea where that was, but he could find out. Then he could rescue Tracy, and ruin Dr. No's mad plans as well!

He looked below him at the buildings and streets of Tokyo. He was beginning to enjoy his trip over the city. "What a view," he said. Then he looked back and frowned. "What a pain!"

Three hang gliders manned by Dr. No's Ninjas were right behind him.

James discovered that by twisting the bar he was holding, he could steer the kite. He angled downward and his speed increased. Ahead of him was a tower of some kind with a metal framework and observation deck. James zoomed in low over the structure.

The tourists didn't see what was happening until James flew across the deck. With wild yells, they dove out of his way.

"Heads up!" James yelled, barely making it through the framework. Then he was out the other side.

Before the tourists could move, two hang gliders followed the kite. They quickly flew through the open-air deck behind James. The third hang glider was not so lucky. As the Ninja guided the glider into the room, the tip of its wing smacked into the ceiling. The glider instantly slammed down into a pile on the floor.

James's kite was starting to sink slowly. He risked a glance backward. Only two Ninjas left on his tail! The odds were improving.

He was about fifty feet in the air, directly above a cluster of cherry trees. He angled toward the trees, and chanced another look over his shoulder. Both hang gliders were still following him, and they were closing in.

He zipped past the upper branches of the cherry trees. The two Ninjas, frantically trying to catch up, were losing control of the hang gliders. In an attempt to cut off James's kite, one of them came in way low. *Way* too low.

James heard a loud *crunch* and looked back. The glider had crashed into a tree. Its pilot was caught in the branches, swaying back and forth.

"Guess that's why they're called *hang* gliders," James muttered.

There was just one Ninja left, but James was still losing altitude. If he landed now, he'd be a sitting duck.

Suddenly, the trees disappeared and James flew over a network of train tracks. A commuter train was humming along right beneath him. James aimed his kite for the roof of the train and then let go.

"Have a nice flight!" he yelled at the last Ninja.

The man, knowing what his punishment would be

if James escaped, swooped down. He landed on the roof of the next car but got tangled in his glider.

Then he screamed.

James had dropped to the roof of the train as it hurtled into a tunnel. The terrified Ninja didn't have time to duck, especially since he was caught up in the glider. The wrecked glider—and the Ninja— slammed into the bricks.

When he reached the other side of the tunnel, James turned around. Except for a few shreds of fabric from the glider, the roof of the next car was empty. "That must have been his stop," he said. In a few minutes the train drew into a station and hissed to a halt. There was only one person waiting to get on. He stared in astonishment as James jumped down from the roof of the car.

"It was too stuffy inside," James said with a grin.

James checked his pocket guide to Tokyo and then shook his head. "What do you know? This *is* my stop!"

He left the station and made his way back to their hotel. The room he was sharing with IQ and Gordo was empty, and there was a note on the table. It was from IQ, explaining that they had gone to the all-night library to read everything they could find about the Kawa Company—and the stolen sword.

"I guess I'd better save them the trouble," James muttered. He turned to leave the room and found his way blocked by a Ninja.

"I've been looking for you," the Ninja said.

Chapter Twelve
Friend or Enemy?

James sighed. It was one of those nights. He fell into a fighting stance, ready to attack. "Wait!" The Ninja held up a hand. "I'm on your side." The hand went to the mask over the Ninja's face and pulled it free.

A young girl shook down her long, dark hair and flashed James a familiar, friendly smile. "Professor Tanaka's secretary!" James exclaimed.

"Actually, I am his daughter." She gave a slight bow. "My name is Sakura. It means Cherry Blossom. My friends call me Cherri."

"Well, I hope we can be friends, Cherri," James replied. "But what are you doing dressed like that?"

Cherri reached behind her and removed a backpack. She took out IQ's mini crossbow and handed it to James. "Saving your life, for one thing. Did you think that all Ninjas were men? Or worked for Dr. No? Or did evil instead of good? For several generations, my family has taken *ninjutsu*—the Ninja discipline—and used it for good ends, not to kill."

James nodded. "So you're the one who fired that arrow. But how did you know where I was?"

"One of the arts of the Ninja is invisibility," she replied with a smile.

"Don't tell me you've been following me around invisibly," James said.

"Hardly that." Cherri laughed. "Invisibility may be simply not being seen for what you are. One of my other arts is that of traditional cooking—and serving."

"You were the geisha in the restaurant!" James realized. "I thought she looked familiar!" Then he frowned. "But why did you disguise yourself like that?"

"Because at first I did not trust you," she said simply. "You came to the museum with a picture of a stolen sword. You went to see my father, and he was then kidnapped. I had no clue as to who had taken him except for you. So I decided to keep track of you and see if you led me to my father."

"I guess if I were you, I'd have suspected me, too," James agreed.

"When you went to the Kawa Company," she went on, "I had thought it was because you were a crook, in league with the Yakuza. I saw you breaking in, and then Dr. No's Ninjas tried to kill you. Then I knew you were on my side." She gave him another dazzling smile. "I am very happy that they did not succeed in killing you."

"Believe me, so am I."

There was a sudden noise and the door swung open.

"James!" cried Phoebe as she, IQ, and Gordo came in. Then she caught sight of Cherri. "And who is this?" she asked icily, glaring at the intruder.

"Um, hi, guys," James answered. "This is Cherri— Professor Tanaka's daughter."

"Oh, really?" Phoebe said, glaring at the Japanese girl. "Are you sure we can trust her?"

"Believe me," James replied, "she has impeccable qualifications."

"Hey! A Ninja dudette!" Gordo exclaimed as he took in Cherri's outfit. "Way cool!"

James told his friends about what had happened at the Kawa building. Then IQ showed James what they had found.

"It's not much," IQ said. "The Kawa Company keeps a very low profile. They avoid publicity."

"Dr. No isn't very newsworthy," James agreed. "So, what about the sword?"

IQ pushed his glasses up the bridge of his nose. "As we know, it's made from meteoric iron. And it seems that the sword was made from a meteorite that fell somewhere about here." He tapped a map of the Japanese islands. "Somewhere to the south, near the island of O-Shima."

"I heard Dr. No mention O-Shima," James said slowly. "Where is it?"

Cherri pointed out the island on the map. "It isn't too far off the coast. I have an uncle who rents out boats in Shimoda. I am certain he will loan us one."

"Awesome! Maybe we could borrow some water skis, too," Gordo suggested. "A windsurfer, even! Cherri, lead the way!"

Mr. Milbanks had a terrible headache. He'd spent all morning trying to arrange class schedules for the next year.

It was his least favorite job. In fact, he hated it. It seemed like every time he fixed one problem, another cropped up. If he moved tenth-grade gym to four o'clock on Fridays, then Mr. Mitchell couldn't possibly teach the eleventh-grade golf class at the same time. Aaargh!

There was a knock on the door. Just what he needed—another problem.

"Come in!" he yelled. He groaned when he saw Trevor Noseworthy. Trevor was constantly running to him with silly stories about James Bond Jr. "Now what?" the headmaster sighed. "More news about Bond?"

"How did you ever know, sir?" Trevor asked.

"Just a wild guess," replied the headmaster. "Well, out with it."

"It's Japan . . . ," Trevor began with a smirk.

Dr. No's sleek black yacht pulled slowly to rest in O-Shima harbor. The yacht was sixty feet long and built for speed. It was one of Dr. No's favorite toys.

81

It could outrace almost any boat in the world. It was also armed with hidden weapons. Dr. No used it as a pleasure craft—and his greatest joy was smuggling stolen goods into and out of Japan.

On the bridge, Dr. No raised a pair of binoculars to his eyes. Morning was just breaking, but Dr. No wasn't interested in the beautiful sky.

"Ah!" he sighed. "I see the Cave of the Temple, just as you said, Professor." He smiled at Professor Tanaka. "So far, it appears that you've been telling me the truth."

"I wish I hadn't," the Professor said defiantly. "But while that young lady's life depends upon me, I have very little choice."

"I'm so glad you realize that," Dr. No answered. He nodded to one of his Ninjas, who took the Professor outside. When he was certain that the old man wouldn't overhear him, Dr. No turned to another of his assassins.

"I hate loose ends," he said coldly. "I suggest you let Miss Milbanks go for a swim. So it isn't too easy for her, why don't you tie her hands and feet first?"

Chapter Thirteen
The Rescue

James looked at his watch and sighed. "Dr. No is bound to be there by now."

Cherri was at the helm of the powerful speedboat that her uncle had loaned her. She pushed the throttle to full power and they roared across the quiet sea. In the distance they could see the outline of the island of O-Shima. "We shall also be there in a short while," she told him.

"I know," James agreed. "But Dr. No is utterly ruthless. Once he has no further need for Tracy and your father, he'll kill them without a second thought. As soon as he reaches that meteorite they'll both be dead."

IQ was clutching the edge of the seat behind James. He looked green and very unhappy. The up-and-down motion of the boat as it hit the waves made him ill.

"Don't worry, James," he managed to say. "I'm sure we'll make it in time."

"Speaking of time," Gordo added, "isn't it time for breakfast? I'm starving." He turned to look through the lockers that lined the side of the boat. "Hey—I wonder if there's food in any of them." He opened the first one, and a big grin creased his face. "Cool! Water skis!"

James shook his head. "I don't care how hungry you are," he joked. "Even you couldn't eat them."

"Hey, we'll still have this righteous boat *after* we nab Tracy and the Prof, right?"

Phoebe looked at him and shook her head. "Concentrate on the rescue first," she suggested. "Tracy must be at her wits' end by now."

Tracy had been dragged from the cabin where she'd been held captive for twelve hours and onto the deck of Dr. No's yacht. There were only two Ninjas left aboard with her, but they were more than enough.

"What are you doing to me?" she yelled.

"It's a nice day," one of the men said smoothly. "We thought you'd like a swim."

"No, thanks," Tracy told him. "I didn't bring my suit."

The other Ninja laughed. "Don't worry—we've got the perfect one for you." He dragged her over to a pile of chains. "Hold out your hands."

When Tracy tried to pull away, he whipped out his deadly sword. "Hold them out, or else!" The men began to wrap the chains around Tracy's hands and feet.

Tracy closed her eyes. She knew what the Ninjas were up to. They were going to drop her over the side, and the weight of the chains would pull her under the water.

In the speedboat Phoebe was staring out over the sea through a pair of binoculars. They were approaching the island.

"There's a yacht ahead of us," she told James. "It's painted black."

"It must be Dr. No's ship," James replied. "He likes that color—it matches his heart."

"James!" Phoebe cried. "You're right! I can see Tracy!"

"Is she all right?" IQ asked.

Phoebe shook her head. "Not unless you think that being tied up in chains and lowered into the bay is all right!"

James grabbed the binoculars from Phoebe and examined the scene. He could see the two Ninjas. They had a small crane and were swinging it over the side of the yacht. At the end of the crane, Tracy was suspended over the water. Fighting down his fear, James turned to his friends. "Gordo, it looks like you're going to get your chance to do some water skiing after all!"

"*Sayonara!*" one of the Ninjas called to Tracy.

The second man pointed out to sea. "Look!" he cried.

Tracy managed to twist around to see what had caught his attention. It was a speedboat pulling a water-skier.

"Tourists," one of the Ninjas complained. "Better get rid of her now." He slammed down the crane's release. With a scream, Tracy fell toward the water.

A huge wave passed over Tracy's head as the speedboat roared by the ship. Then Tracy felt a strong arm around her waist, scooping her out of the water.

"Hey!" she heard Gordo say. "I just made the catch of the day." Tracy opened her eyes and looked at his grinning face. Then he frowned. "It's a bit small—maybe I should throw it back."

"Don't you dare!" Tracy looked up, and saw Phoebe and IQ waving at her from the speedboat.

"But where's James?" she asked Gordo.

James came up out of the water on the far side of the yacht. Hand over hand, he hauled himself up by the ship's anchor chain. The small oxygen tank that IQ had given him worked perfectly. It looked like a slim metal tube and clipped around his neck. It supposedly held enough air for thirty minutes underwater. Using it, James had swum underwater without being detected by the guards. Now, with a little luck, they'd be too busy concentrating on Gordo's rescue of Tracy to notice that he'd come aboard.

He made it to the deck and paused to check out the situation. He could see only two Ninjas, both of them furiously yelling at James's friends in the speed-

boat. It wasn't hard to imagine what the two guards were upset about.

James found a fishing net neatly piled on the deck. The Ninjas didn't even hear him coming. They were too busy fighting over how to recapture Tracy. They knew what their fate would be if Dr. No found out that they hadn't managed to kill her.

"The laser cannon," one of them growled. "We can use it to get the boat!" He turned to the controls.

James dropped the net over them and drew it tight.

The Ninjas were tied up neat as a pouch. Just to be sure, James pulled the rope ends even tighter. Unhappy Ninja yells and hollers erupted all over again. It was music to James's ears.

James slipped the end of the rope through a pulley and hoisted them off the deck.

"I believe there's a law against keeping this species," he said. "I'd better just toss them back." He pushed the net toward the guard rail and dumped the Ninjas into the churning water.

James did a quick search of the yacht while he waited for the speedboat to come back. There wasn't anyone else on board, so James figured that Dr. No and Professor Tanaka were already on the island. Cherri pulled up alongside the yacht, and James jumped down next to Tracy.

"Am I glad to see you," James said, giving Tracy a hug.

"Believe me, James, it's great to be aboard!" Tracy replied. "But as I just told everyone, Dr. No still has

Cherri's father and he knows where the meteorite is. It's in a temple in a cave on the mountain."

Tracy pointed at the largest of the mountains on O-Shima.

"And once he has the meteorite," IQ said glumly, "he'll have the power to destroy the world."

Chapter Fourteen
The Temple in the Mountain

Dr. No seemed to be completely unaffected by the long climb up the mountain. Eager to reach the meteorite, it took all of his self-control to wait for the elderly Professor. "Unlimited power is almost within my grasp!" he exclaimed. "Will you get a move on?"

"I'm doing the best I can," the old man replied between gasps. "But I'm not up to this effort."

"You'd better be," Dr. No hissed. "This is the entrance to the temple, come on!" He led the way into the cave opening. "Follow me at once!" he ordered in exasperation.

They soon reached the main chamber of the temple. It was a huge natural cavern, its ceiling about a hundred and fifty feet over their heads. Torches, placed on rocky outcroppings and ledges along the cavern's walls by the monks who tended the temple, gave off a flickering light. There were no monks or pilgrims in the temple this early in the day; the footsteps of Dr. No and Professor Tanaka echoed hollowly in the empty stone chamber.

In the center of the cavern was a huge statue of the Buddha. It was carved from stone, and its eyes faced the entrance to the cave. The Buddha was about sixty feet tall and had an old stone altar in front of it. Ancient rocks cut into the shapes of animals were scattered around the base of the statue. But there was no sign of the meteorite.

Dr. No turned back to Professor Tanaka. "Where is the meteorite?" he snarled. "I don't see it—and I must have it!"

The Professor shook his head. "The inscription on the sword does not say. It merely claims that the meteorite is here, in this temple."

"In that case," Dr. No. said coldly, "I have no further need of you." He grabbed two of the Ninjas. "Search this temple and find the meteorite!" As they started off he turned to the two men who were holding the Professor. "As for him, he can go now."

Professor Tanaka looked astounded. "You're letting me go?"

"Yes, Professor." Then the villain smiled. It was a very nasty smile. "But I am worried that the climb down might exhaust you." To his Ninjas he added, "Show him the shortcut down—over the cliff!"

The two Ninjas laughed while they dragged the

struggling old man back through the passageway. Dr. No turned back to the Buddha, his eyes blazing with greed. "I must have that meteorite!"

Professor Tanaka was still struggling as the Ninjas pulled him out onto a ledge. They enjoyed this part of their job. One of them grabbed the Professor by his collar and prepared to swing him over the edge of the cliff.

At that second, a girl dressed completely in black suddenly leaped into their way. She was twirling a set of *nunchakus*—two short sticks joined by a length of chain. She wore no mask, and the hatred on her face was quite clear.

"Let him go," she whispered dangerously.

The two Ninjas looked at each other and then nodded. They tossed the Professor aside and he fell to the ground, watching in disbelief.

The Ninjas yelled and leaped at the girl. She rolled forward under their jump and whirled the *nunchakus* through the air. They wrapped around the ankle of one of the Ninjas, and she gave them a sharp tug. Yanked off balance, the Ninja's leg twisted under him and he collapsed. The girl sprang to her feet and whipped around. Her boot lashed out, catching the fallen Ninja under the chin. The force of the blow sent the man flying into a tree. He was knocked out cold.

The other Ninja faced the girl. She was weaponless, her *nunchakus* on the ground by the tree. With a low laugh, the remaining Ninja pulled a throwing star from his belt. Viciously, he flung it at the girl's throat.

In a blur of motion, she ducked under the spinning blades. She whirled around and threw a roundhouse kick. The Ninja spun and grabbed her foot. He began twisting her ankle, but suddenly released his grip and fell forward.

Gordo smiled down at the unconscious man and threw down the broken branch he'd hit him with. "Don't you know it's not polite to hit a babe?" he asked. "Excuse me, I meant a Ninja dudette."

Cherri ran over to her father. She offered him a hand, and he looked up at her in astonishment.

"Cherri! What are you doing here?" he gasped.

"Rescuing you, of course," she replied. "As any dutiful daughter would when her father was in danger." She threw her arms about him and hugged him hard.

Gordo laughed. "Man, I just *love* family reunions!"

Professor Tanaka stared at him, and then at IQ, Phoebe, and Tracy as they came running up the path. He pointed to Tracy. "I recognize this young lady from the boat—and I am very happy to see her safe. But who are these other people?"

"They are friends of James Bond Jr.'s," Cherri explained.

Her father frowned. "The young man who came to see me at the temple in Tokyo." He looked around. "But I don't see him. Where is he?"

Cherri pointed toward the cave. "He went after Dr. No."

Chapter Fifteen
The Secret of the Temple

The Ninjas knew that Dr. No would not hesitate to kill them if they did not find the meteorite. But there seemed to be nothing hidden in the temple. All they discovered was a small flock of bats nesting on a dark wall that suddenly burst into flight when one of the men disturbed them.

Dr. No jumped as the bats flew into the air. He had the Yoritomo sword in his hands, ready to strike. Then he realized what had startled him. "Bats!" he snarled in disgust. "Is that all you can find?"

"Yes, master," said the Ninja leader. "The meteorite does not seem to be here."

"It *must* be here!" Dr. No exclaimed. "The map on this sword cannot be wrong. You idiots haven't looked hard enough! Search again—and this time find it, or you'll lose your lives!"

James peered down from a rocky outcropping high above the assassins' heads. He had snuck into the cave and noiselessly climbed up the rough wall while the Ninjas and Dr. No were searching the other end of the cavern. Dr. No was facing away from the Buddha with the stolen sword in his hands.

James got quietly to his feet. "I think it's time to drop in on the Doctor," he murmured to himself. Then he jumped from the edge of the outcropping toward the statue.

As he jumped rock crumbled under his feet and showered down onto the floor of the cavern. James flew through the air and grabbed hold of the neck of the statue.

"What's that?" Dr. No snapped, whirling around. His eyes darted around the cave. "It must have been those stupid bats again."

He turned back to his men. "Well?" he barked, annoyed at the delay.

"Nothing, master," the leader said. "We have searched all over."

Dr. No's eyes narrowed. "I do not tolerate failure!" he cried, bringing the sword up over the Ninja's head.

James was ready for action. He had brought along more of IQ's thin, strong line. He made a loop in the end and threw it like a lasso. As Dr. No raised the sword to strike, the line slipped over it and tightened around its hilt.

"What?" Dr. No howled as the sword was yanked out of his grasp. He looked up and saw James reeling in his catch. "It's young Bond again! Get him, you fools! He has the sword!"

James dove for cover behind the stone head of the Buddha. Several throwing stars whistled past; some clattered off the stone statue.

"You numbskulls!" he heard Dr. No yell. "Use your lasers and bring that thing down around him!"

"Quick-tempered, isn't he?" James commented to the Buddha.

Blasts from the laser rifles started to heat the statue. But James didn't have to hide; he had the Yoritomo sword.

The Ninjas opened fire on James as he jumped out onto the Buddha's shoulder. "Here, Doctor!" he called out. "A taste of your own medicine!"

He raised the sword to block the beams. When they hit the blade, the beams intensified a hundredfold and bounced off. Now blazing beams of destruction, they flashed back to the ground. Small explosions shot up as the beams vaporized rocks and dirt. The ground shook, and the Ninjas dove for cover.

Dr. No was furious. His mighty Ninjas were cowering from this young intruder. He ran toward the statue of the Buddha, flexing his metal hands. First he slammed one hand, then the other, into the stone. His metal fingers dug in deep, giving him the ability to climb up the statue's front.

James didn't see Dr. No until it was almost too late. At virtually the same time he realized that the statue was shaking. He glanced down and saw that the ground was slowly starting to cave in.

96

"Uh-oh," he muttered. "Those amplified blasts must have weakened the cavern floor. Things are getting pretty shaky . . ."

Dr. No was climbing up the Buddah like a fly. When the Doctor had almost made it to the shoulder he reached up with his right claw, aiming for James's ankle. James jumped back, aware that if the claw closed around him, it would crush his foot.

The sudden movement almost sent James tumbling from his perch. He fell to one knee, which gave Dr. No enough time to join him on the huge shoulder. There was hatred and madness burning in the Doctor's eyes as he advanced on James.

"I've had more than enough of your interference," he spat. "This is your final stand, young Bond." He raised his metal hands.

James could hear the powerful motors in Dr. No's hands as they began to close around his neck.

Chapter Sixteen
The Meteorite

James instantly raised the Sword of Death.

Dr. No snarled as his metal claws slammed into the blade. The blow was so powerful that it ripped the sword from James's grip, numbing his fingers.

"This temple is going to be your tomb!" Dr. No growled.

James was beginning to suspect that Dr. No might be right. There was nowhere for him to run and no way to escape the menacing claws.

The ground suddenly shook again and then started to give way. The statue jerked forward, as if it were bowing, and cracks began to split it into large pieces. Dr. No reflexively slammed his left hand out, burying the fingers deep into the stone head of the statue.

"This is a fine time to go to pieces," James muttered

as the stone beneath his feet started to slip out from under him. The hole in the ground was growing larger, and the statue swayed more and more violently. Giving up the losing battle to keep his footing, James leaped clear of the falling Buddha.

By now, the head of the Buddha was only about ten feet from the ground, but James still had the wind knocked out of him. As he struggled to catch his breath and get to his feet, he saw the glint of metal beside him. The sword! He grabbed hold of it and noticed that the line was still attached.

The ground was still trembling, and the part of the floor he'd fallen onto began to slide into the yawning pit. He quickly staggered to his feet and threw the sword with all of his might. His aim was good, and the blade became wedged into a crevice in the cave wall.

James glanced at the statue, which had fragmented into several large pieces in the rumbling collapse of the cavern's floor. He saw Dr. No struggling to pull his claw out of the stone head, but it was embedded too deeply. With a scream, the Doctor was dragged into the abyss. There was no sign of his Ninja warriors. They must have tumbled into the pit or fled outside to safety.

The line in James's hand tightened as the ground beneath him fell away. The amplified laser blasts must have caused the cavern's floor to collapse into another cave beneath it. He swung on the end of the rope and looked about the shattered temple.

Not all of the floor had collapsed. The area where

the statue had been was still intact. And there, where the Buddha had sat for hundreds of years—

"James!"

He looked up and grinned. Tracy was kneeling at the edge of the drop, staring down at him.

"What are you doing?" she called.

"Just hanging around," he answered.

"Hold on," she said. "We'll pull you up."

James was soon standing on firm ground again. He looked around, pleased that they had all made it safely. Then he pointed to the spot where the statue had once stood.

"There's what Dr. No was after," he said. "The monks who carved the statue of the Buddha knew that the meteorite was too powerful to be used without great wisdom. So they hollowed out the base of the statue and placed it right over the meteorite.

They all looked where he was pointing.

The meteorite didn't look like much—just a huge lump of blackened rock. There was one section where a chunk had been chipped off. It must have been used to make the two swords.

"It must weigh *tons!*" IQ said in awe. "Imagine what damage Dr. No could have done if he'd gotten his hands on that!"

"Yes," James agreed. "And he almost got his hands on me. It was a close thing."

Cherri gazed down into the pit. The rumbling had finally stopped. The gaping hole was about thirty feet deep but there was little to see at the bottom except for rubble.

James worked the Yoritomo sword from the crevice and carefully handed it to Professor Tanaka. "Perhaps you could return this to the proper authorities," he suggested. "I might have some trouble explaining how I got my hands on it."

"Certainly," he agreed with a smile.

"James," Cherri called out. "What happened to Dr. No?"

"He fell into the pit," James replied. He glanced down and then realized there was no sign of the villain. "Maybe the cavern below also has an opening onto the face of the mountain . . ."

They all ran outside.

About a quarter of a mile down the mountainside, Dr. No and his three remaining Ninjas were running for their lives.

"Come on," James said grimly. "After what he's done, we can't let him get away."

Chapter Seventeen
Battle at Sea

James and his friends sprinted down the mountain toward the harbor. Professor Tanaka fell behind, clutching the Yoritomo sword carefully to his chest.

"Go on without me!" he called. "I will only slow you down."

The rest of them rushed onward, but Dr. No and his men reached their small boat on the beach before James and his companions could cut them off. Dr. No and the Ninjas were already headed back to the yacht when James struck out for the speedboat. His friends were right behind him.

"James," Tracy said after they'd all leaped aboard, "that yacht of Dr. No's is armed to the teeth. He's got laser cannons built into it and everything. If they get there, we're sunk—literally!"

"Bogus," Gordo muttered.

As Cherri sent the speedboat surging through the choppy water James turned to IQ. "You wouldn't have anything that might be of use, would you?"

IQ blinked. "Not to take on a battleship, James."

"Don't worry about it," James said. "Just give me what you've got."

IQ rummaged through the bag he'd left in the boat. "Just the mini crossbow, my alarm detectors, the infrared sunglasses, my small line-shooting gun, the—"

"Hold it," James said. He grabbed the crossbow and one of the bolts. Then he turned to Tracy. "See if this boat has a flare gun in the locker," he suggested. "Maybe I can put a hole in Dr. No's plans."

"I like it!" Gordo said. "The old flare-gun-and-boat-fuel-explosion bit. Didn't we use that against Skullcap?"

"Exactly," James agreed. "If it worked once, why not try it again?" He moved up next to Cherri. They were now only a couple of hundred yards from Dr. No's boat. "Try to keep us steady," he told her. Then he jumped onto the prow of the boat and lay down flat. He aimed the crossbow carefully and fired.

The bolt flew straight and slammed into the small boat's outboard motor, penetrating the fuel tank.

"Bull's-eye!" James said with a grin, seeing the gas leaking from the hole. "That should slow him down!"

Tracy held a flare gun in her hand. "Cherri's uncle keeps this boat well stocked," she said, handing James the gun.

104

"Terrific. I think it's time we turned the heat on Dr. No."

"Too late!" Cherri called. She pointed.

Despite the leak from the boat, Dr. No had made it to his yacht. He and the Ninjas were climbing up the ladder to the deck.

"Maybe not," James answered. He aimed and fired.

The blazing flare skipped across the water before impacting with the leaking outboard motor. There was a terrific roar and a ball of fire exploded out of the boat. The villains on the yacht threw themselves to the deck as the smaller boat cracked in two and started to sink. Reeling away from the flames and smoke, Dr. No rushed into the yacht's cabin and started the engines.

"Trouble," James said softly as he spotted the Ninjas running toward the laser cannons.

"I'll say," Tracy agreed.

James saw that the small boat was blazing away and had flipped over. Most of it was underwater. Dr. No's yacht began to pull away from it.

"If he gets going," James said, "he should easily be able to outrun us. Cherri, take us back around again. Okay?"

"Of course, James," she agreed. "But what do you have in mind?"

He grinned at her. "I think it's time I took up one of Gordo's favorite sports."

The three Ninjas worked quickly, raising one of the cannons and securing it into place on the deck. One of them powered it up while the other two searched for their target.

"There!" the leader called out. "They're coming back."

"I don't believe it," the Ninja manning the laser muttered. "They're towing a water-skier!"

The man at the controls grinned. "It'll be just like shooting a sitting duck!"

James was being towed behind the speedboat, heading straight for the blazing wreckage of the sinking boat. The sloping bottom of the boat would make a perfect ramp to launch him into the air . . . except for the fact that it was still on fire.

James knew that if you were fast enough you could pass your finger through the flame of a candle without getting burned. He should be able to pass through the flames here—if he was fast enough. Of course, if he wasn't going at the right speed . . .

Cherri was picking up speed and would have to swing around in a moment—or the speedboat might crash into the wreck. Beyond the dancing flames, James could see the Ninjas on the deck of Dr. No's yacht.

With only inches to spare, Cherri swung hard to the right. All James could see were flames, and then he was surrounded by them. His skis hit the boat and he was airborne.

He released the tow rope as he came to the peak of his leap and sailed right onto the deck of Dr. No's yacht. Luckily he had moved through the inferno at the right speed.

The three Ninjas were taken totally by surprise. They had never seen anything this crazy—or dangerous. They barely had time to react before James smacked into them. The laser cannon was knocked free and swung around just as it opened fire.

Its intense beam sliced through the cabin, setting the wooden frame ablaze. Dr. No screamed and dove for the floor as the beam narrowly missed his head.

Meanwhile James had hit the deck and was skiing across the polished wood. He heard a small explosion and risked a quick look over his shoulder.

Still firing, the laser was slowly swinging back in the other direction. Finally it returned to its home position—pointing straight down.

"That should give Dr. No a sinking feeling," James remarked to himself. Then, just as he approached the yacht's safety rail, he slipped his feet out of the skis and dove overboard.

Tracy was trying to follow the action with IQ's binoculars. She was telling the others in the speedboat what was happening on Dr. No's yacht.

"The laser's taken the top off the cabin," Tracy reported. "Now it's burning a hole in the bilges, or whatever they call that part at the bottom of the boat. James has just gone over the side, and—"

There was a sudden blast of flame and the yacht exploded.

"James!" Tracy screamed.

Chapter Eighteen
Home, James

Tracy stared over the side of the speedboat at the water. Cherri slowly circled their boat around the blazing wreckage that had been Dr. No's yacht.

IQ shook his head. "Not only is there no sign of James, Dr. No and his Ninjas seem to have disappeared as well."

"James can't be dead," Phoebe cried. "He can't be!"

"That's right," said James's voice from the rear of the boat. "I only feel half dead."

They all spun around to see him climbing aboard. Gordo grabbed his arms and dragged him into the boat.

"What do you mean, scaring us all like that?" Tracy demanded.

James lay down on the deck and sighed. "I'd have caught up with you faster if you hadn't been going in circles. I got pretty dizzy trying to get aboard." He looked over at IQ. "Oh, you were wrong about your mini oxygen tank."

"I was?" IQ asked.

"It doesn't have thirty minutes of air in it. Only twenty-seven."

"Oh." IQ frowned. "I'll have to recalibrate it."

Cherri smiled at James. "Well, that's the last trouble we'll have from Dr. No, at least."

"Don't be so certain," James replied. "When I was underwater, something passed under me. I can't be sure, but it looked like a small submarine." Then he shook his head. "I was so groggy from the blast. Maybe I just imagined it."

Tracy stared over the side of the speedboat, watching the debris of Dr. No's yacht burn. "As far as Dr. No goes," she said, "I wouldn't put anything past him."

"As far as Dr. No goes," Gordo said, "the farther, the better!"

Later that day, Professor Tanaka and Cherri insisted on seeing James and his friends off at the Tokyo airport.

"You have done Japan a great service," the Professor told them. "And we are truly grateful. I shall ensure that the sword is returned to the traveling exhibition. And I have already begun preparations for my government to recover the meteorite. I will guarantee that it will be put to good use—not to the criminal purposes of villains like Dr. No."

"There is even better news, I think," Cherri said, smiling. "The Buddha was not as badly damaged by its mistreatment as we thought. It is being restored and will soon be back where it belongs—in the temple. So as you say, we have our cake and can eat it, too. The Buddha restored and—"

"The meteorite," her father finished.

"There can be no better hands to leave such treasures in," James said. "It has been an honor to meet and help you, sir." He turned to Cherri. "And a pleasure to know you."

As they walked across the terminal for their flight, Tracy looked at Gordo's glum face. "What's with you?" she asked.

"I'm just hoping there are no dogs on this flight," Gordo replied. "Phoebe's connections were bad news on the way here."

"This isn't one of Phoebe's flights, Gordo," IQ broke in. "This one is on Professor Tanaka—first class on a jumbo jet."

Gordo looked up and his face changed. "Hey, maybe there *is* something to this saving-the-world gig after all! What's the in-flight movie?"

Back at Warfield Academy, James finally told Tracy how Trevor had overheard their plans and threatened to tell her father.

"We've been gone three days," he said glumly. "Your father must know by now that you were kidnapped and that we went off to Japan after you. He'll

111

probably ground you for the rest of your life—and expel me."

"If he wants to expel you," Tracy told him, "then he'd better be prepared to expel me, too. I, for one, appreciate your rescue." She patted his arm. "Anyway, for all his gruffness, Daddy really loves me. He's bound to take into consideration that you *did* save me from Dr. No."

"That's why I think he'll just expel me instead of having me shot at dawn."

They had walked as slowly as they could drag their feet. Still, they were finally standing in front of the headmaster's door. Witih a deep sigh, James reached out and knocked.

"Now what?" came Mr. Milbanks's voice. "Come in!"

He didn't sound like he was in a good mood. It took all of James's courage to open the door and march inside. Tracy walked in beside him, bravely ready to share his fate.

"What the blazes do you two want?" asked the headmaster. "I'm in the middle of planning next year's class schedules."

James stared at Mr. Milbanks. He seemed to be angry, all right, but only at being interrupted. "Ah . . . have you spoken with Trevor Noseworthy recently?"

"Yes, I have," the headmaster grumbled. "And I assume you're both feeling better now."

"Better?" asked Tracy faintly.

"Yes, better." The headmaster stared at his daughter. "You are over it, I hope. Otherwise you'd better get back to bed this instant."

James had no idea what was going on. It was quite clear, however, that whatever Trevor had told Mr. Milbanks, they were both off the hook. "Ah . . . yes, we're perfectly well, sir."

"Good." The headmaster turned back to his schedule. "Well, run along, then."

When they were outside the office, Tracy turned to James. "Do you have any idea what he was talking about?"

"None at all," James admitted.

"I may be able to shed a little light on things."

James and Tracy turned around to see Mr. Mitchell smiling down at them. The gym teacher scratched his head. "Poor old Trevor was so exhausted after that eight-mile run that he . . . um, *volunteered* for, that he fell asleep. It seems that when he woke up, he'd somehow gotten his facts all confused. Instead of telling Mr. Milbanks that you had *flown* to Japan, he said something about you all having the Japan ese flu."

James stared at Mr. Mitchell. "I wonder what gave him that idea?"

The teacher shrugged. "With Trevor, who knows?" He smiled and walked off down the corridor.

Tracy grabbed James's arm and pointed. "Look," she whispered.

In the teacher's back pocket was a book. James could just make out the title: *Hypnotism Made Easy*.

Look for these exciting JAMES BOND JR. adventures:

#1 A View to a Thrill   The dastardly Scumlord is scheming to steal a top-secret device—and kidnap James! James is already in the thick of a spy caper, and it's only the first day of school!

#2 The Eiffel Target   The foul Dr. Derange has planted a nuclear bomb in the Eiffel Tower! Can James sneak to Paris and dismantle the warhead?

#3 Live and Let's Dance   James is in a deadly race against the clock! If he doesn't get to Switzerland in time, the notorious arms dealer Baron von Skarin will assassinate the heir to the throne of Zamora.

#4 Sandblast!   The evil Pharaoh Fearo is trying to buy up the world's supply of oil with stolen treasures. If he succeeds, S.C.U.M. will rule the earth.

JAMES BOND JR.

Contest Rules
Create Your Own James Bond Jr. Villain

1. Mail all entries to: **James Bond Jr. Contest**, Puffin Books, Penguin USA, 375 Hudson Street, New York, NY 10014. One entry per person. 2. All entries must be received by November 1, 1992. 3. The winning entries will be judged as follows: 50% for drawing, 50% for essay. All entries become property of Danjac and UA Corp. and can be used for promotional purposes. The two winners will be notified by mail. 4. This contest is open to all U.S. and Canadian residents between the ages of 8 and 12 as of December 1, 1991. The winners will be announced on February 1, 1993. 5. Two winners will each receive a Nintendo™ system and a **James Bond Jr.** Game Pak, plus an Espionage Kit and a complete **James Bond Jr.** library. Taxes, if any, are the responsibility of the prize winners. Winners' parents/guardians will be required to sign and return a statement of eligibility. Names and addresses of the winners may be used for promotional purposes. 6. No substitution of prizes is permitted. 7. For the name of the prize-winners, send a self-addressed, stamped envelope to: **James Bond Jr. Contest**, Puffin Books Marketing Dept., Penguin USA, 375 Hudson Street, New York, NY 10014.

The James Bond Jr.
Create a Villain Contest

Puffin is pleased to announce the **James Bond Jr.** contest that could win you a Nintendo™ system and a **James Bond Jr.** Game Pak, plus an Espionage Kit and a complete **James Bond Jr.** library!

Being 007's nephew is glamorous, all right, but it also means running up against some pretty unsavory characters. Submit a drawing plus a 200 word or less essay describing the most despicable, low-down bounder ever to disgrace the world of espionage. Please submit your drawing and essay on two separate sheets of white 8 1/2 x 11 paper, and make sure your essay is neatly printed or typewritten. Fill out this coupon completely and staple it to your entry.

Mail your entry to: **James Bond Jr. Contest**
Puffin Books Marketing Dept.
Penguin USA
375 Hudson St.
New York, NY 10014

Name _____ Age _____

Address _____

City/State/Zip _____

Store name (where you saw offer) _____

Store address _____

City/State/Zip _____